Born a **Amy Ruttan** fled the big city to settle down with the country boy of her dreams. After the birth of her second child Amy was lucky enough to realise her lifelong dream of becoming a romance author. When she's not furiously typing away at her computer she's mum to three wonderful children, who use her as a personal taxi and chef.

CARRYING THE SURGEON'S BABY

AMY RUTTAN

MILLS & BOON

First Published in Great Britain 2019
by Mills & Boon, an imprint of HarperCollins*Publishers*
1 London Bridge Street, London, SE1 9GF

© 2019 Amy Ruttan

ISBN: 978-0-263-26959-8

MIX
Paper from
responsible sources
FSC **C007454**

This book is produced from independently certified FSC™ paper
to ensure responsible forest management.
For more information visit www.harpercollins.co.uk/green.

Printed and bound in Spain
by CPI, Barcelona

This book is dedicated to my son Aidan
and to all who see the world in a different way
that the rest of us aren't privileged to see.

PROLOGUE

Las Vegas, Nevada

SHE WASN'T COMPLETELY sure how she'd got here.

"And do you, Dr. Emily West, take Dr. Ryan Gary as your lawfully wedded husband?"

"Yep!" she said brightly, and she narrowed her eyes to get a better look at the Elvis impersonator standing in front of her. She couldn't figure out why he was slightly sideways.

This is the most irrational thing I've ever done.

At least that's what she thought, but Emily wasn't completely clear right now. She glanced over at the man standing next to her and a silly grin spread across her face.

She didn't know how she'd ended up in this wedding chapel with the most eligible, sexiest, charming neurosurgeon in the world, but right now she wasn't feeling any pain. Which was good. Usually, she struggled with anxiety in any kind of social situation. It had been hard to attend his lecture on conjoined twins and then to talk to Dr. Ryan West after the lecture to tell him how much she admired his work.

After her relationship with Robert, another surgeon,

had crashed and burned because of professional jealousy, the last thing she had expected was Ryan asking her for a drink. She'd told herself she shouldn't, but had then thought one drink with a colleague couldn't hurt.

It had been the other five that had hurt, but the more they'd talked about surgery and the conference, the more she'd felt comfortable around him.

She certainly hadn't expected a marriage proposal either. At least, that's what she thought had happened. It had been dinner, dancing, drinks and then making out in the back of his hired car. Now they were here, in a chapel off the strip.

And he was sort of leaning to one side too.

What is happening here? When did you lose control?

Emily smiled to herself. It was kind of fun to let loose. She never did have any fun. She hadn't dated after her relationship with Robert had ended. She'd had no interest in other men and really didn't understand the social nuances of dating, so she didn't bother.

But then Ryan had seemed just as keen about her work as she was about his. And his smile, his confidence just made her completely weak in the knees.

Being around Ryan made her lose control.

"And do you, Dr. Ryan Gary, take Dr. Emily West as your lawfully wedded wife?"

"What?" he asked, leaning in a bit closer and squinting those bright blue eyes that had twinkled at her when they were having dinner.

Maybe it wasn't her spinning, but Ryan who was doing the spinning. She closed her eyes for a moment but could still feel the room spinning. Maybe it was both of them.

The Elvis looked concerned.

"Of course! Of course I do." Ryan grinned at her and she felt her knees go weak. Again, that could be from the mojitos. At least she'd thought it was a mojito.

"Then by the power vested in me by the State of Nevada, I now pronounce you man and wife."

Emily threw her bouquet at the Elvis and Ryan scooped her up in his arms.

"This is the craziest thing I've ever done," he said breathlessly as he carried her down the aisle.

"I think you're supposed to carry me over the threshold and not down the aisle."

"You're light as a feather," he whispered against her ear. A zing of electricity raced down her spine. Then he teetered slightly to the right and set her down. "Perhaps I should wait until the hotel room to carry you over the threshold. Those mojitos were strong."

Emily laughed because he had said the word mojito again.

"What's so funny?" he asked as he slipped his arm around her and they walked over to the hired car.

"Mojito is a funny word."

"What?"

"You know when you say a word a lot it's funny?"

"Mojito," he said again, emphasizing the *mo* in the mojito.

Emily giggled.

The driver cocked an eyebrow as he opened the back door of the town car and they climbed in. Ryan was still chuckling.

"Man, those drinks were strong! I have a flight tomorrow…or is that today?" He glanced at his wrist.

"Today. I think it's after midnight."

He grinned lazily at her, making her heart skip a beat. "Does that mean you're going to turn into a pumpkin?"

"Nope. Are you?"

He touched her cheek and kissed her. It was hot, heavy and in that kiss it all made sense. And suddenly she wasn't questioning her decision to marry Ryan when he'd asked.

It felt so right and she hadn't felt right with a man in a long, long time.

And Robert had never, ever had made her *want* someone this bad before.

He touched her cheek again. "I'm glad I asked you out to dinner and I'm glad we got married."

Emily giggled again. "What happens in Vegas stays in Vegas, right?"

"Right!"

The car pulled up in front of the hotel. Ryan slipped out first after the driver opened the door for them.

"You sure you're okay, Dr. West and Dr. Gary?" the driver asked.

"Couldn't be better," Ryan said.

Emily nodded. "This is awesome!"

And she wasn't particularly sure if she'd used the word awesome before, but she liked the way that sounded, just as much as she liked the way mojito sounded. It rolled off the tongue.

The driver raised his eyebrows and then nodded.

Ryan slipped his arm around her and they walked into the hotel. They took the elevator up to his suite and Emily helped him open the door, as he was fumbling a bit with the card. When the door was open, he bent down and scooped her up in his arms.

Her pulse was racing. Anticipation coursing through

her. This felt right. She wanted this. Maybe doing this would help her to move on.

"You're sure?" Ryan asked, his blue eyes twinkling as he held her close.

"So sure." She kissed him, running her hands through the hair at the nape of his neck. "I want this, Ryan. If I didn't want this I wouldn't be here."

He smiled at her. "Then let me carry you over the threshold, wife."

Emily felt giddy.

It was just one night. What harm could one night cause?

CHAPTER ONE

Seattle, six months later

"Wow." EMILY LOOKED again at the ultrasound scan that her colleague Dr. Ruchi had sent her from her hospital, which was in a small town that was sandwiched between Portland and Seattle. She leaned back in her chair and stared at the ultrasound again.

"Yeah, the conjoined twins have two separate spines, they share a lot of nerves at the base of the spine. They also share a liver, part of their colon and there are three kidneys between the two babies."

"I'm glad to see they have four fully formed limbs and separate genitalia."

Dissecting a liver and separation was easier when the separation gave each twin the chance of being able to survive on their own. The twins didn't share a heart or a brain, and shared organs that could easily be split. It was promising, risky but promising.

It was whether or not all limbs would be fully functional or whether the twins survived their birth. That was the scary part, surviving.

"Yes, that is a positive," Dr. Ruchi said.

"And the parents have consented to being moved up

to Seattle and me preforming the surgery?" Emily asked as she zoomed in on the most recent scan of the babies in utero.

"Yes. The mother was informed that her twins were conjoined and she was given all the details about the risks of separating them postdelivery, but chose to proceed with the birth."

Emily felt a faint kick and looked down at her belly. At six months pregnant there was no longer any hiding her baby bump. And it hit her hard when Dr. Ruchi said that the patient had chosen to proceed with the birth. What a hard decision for a mother to make. She was glad that she didn't have to be put in that position to make a choice. Her baby was, so far, healthy.

"When are you planning to deliver them?"

"Well, I'm not. I would rather send the parents up to Seattle and have her in your care. My hope is that the mother remains on bed rest with yourselves pending a delivery by C-section in a few weeks, once the babies are more developed. It's important that the twins are delivered there so they can benefit from your immediate expertise. You're one of the best pediatric surgeons in the country and have done successful separations before."

"Sure, of course. I would be happy to, but my concern is about the bundle of nerves that the twins share. That worries me. I can work with them on separating the liver and kidneys, even the colon, but for the nerves I would need a world-class neurosurgeon who was familiar with this kind of work to assist me with that part of the operation."

"I have a neurosurgeon for you."

As soon as Dr. Ruchi said the words, Emily's stomach did a flip, a flop and then nose-dived to the bottom of her shoes and she found herself trying not to let her breakfast make a second appearance.

"You…what?" Emily asked, relieved that Dr. Ruchi could not see her expression over the phone, because she knew exactly who Dr. Ruchi was referring to.

"Dr. Ryan Gary. He's agreed to fly to Seattle from San Diego and help with the case. This is my patient, I delivered her first child and I really want you and Dr. Gary to handle the separation."

Dr. Ruchi was right about Ryan. He was the best. He'd done separations before. She just didn't know if working with a man she had just sent divorce papers to would be a touch too awkward.

Her previous relationship had ended badly. So badly it had crushed her. Which was why Emily had been wary of getting into any kind of personal relationship with another surgeon.

Not just wary…determined she was never going to again. So her one-night stand with Dr. Ryan Gary had been a huge mistake. It had been an amazing night, but it had been bad for her afterwards. She was pregnant and alone. She regretted it.

No, you don't.

She wasn't going to disappoint Dr. Ruchi by telling her that she couldn't work with Dr. Ryan Gary because he'd been the one to knock her up after a drunken night in Las Vegas. That night in Vegas had been the biggest mistake of her life.

And when she'd reached out to Ryan to tell him about the baby, she'd found he'd left for a tour of duty providing medical aid abroad in war-torn countries. He'd never responded to her, even when she'd sent him divorce papers.

Which was fine. She'd get the divorce finalized one way or another.

Emily hadn't planned to have a family now, or raise a baby alone, but waiting around for Ryan to respond to her wasn't going to stop her from doing just that.

"Emily, are you okay?" Dr. Ruchi asked, interrupting her train of thoughts.

"What?" she asked. "Yes, sorry. Dr. Gary, you say?"

"Yes. Is there a problem?" Dr. Ruchi asked. Emily could hear the concern in her friend's voice. It had taken Emily years to pick up on social cues like this. She didn't always get them, but since Robert had left her five years ago, and now, on the verge of becoming a single mother, she could tell when someone was concerned about her. She saw it enough in the way people spoke to her, like they felt sorry for her.

"Nope. I might have to clear it with the chief of surgery first. I mean, we do have pretty top-notch neuro-surgeons at SMFPC."

Liar.

Yeah, she did have a problem with his arrival. When he hadn't responded to her emails about being pregnant she'd assumed he'd wanted out.

Emily had been hurt again by a man, but she could raise this baby on her own. She didn't need help. She didn't want Ryan back in her life, but it would be best for the patients. He was an excellent surgeon.

"I've already cleared it with your chief," Dr. Ruchi said gently. "I wanted to make sure that I had you on this case. I didn't want him to pass off my patient to another pediatric surgeon!"

Emily chuckled. "Ana, you know that I'm Head of Pediatrics."

Ana sighed and then laughed. "Okay, so I wanted to make sure that he'd allow Dr. Gary to practice there too."

"And it's okay, I take it?" Emily teased.

"It is. Thank you for doing this, Emily. There's no one else I trust. Both you and Ryan have done separations and done them successfully, with both twins surviving. I know that you can do this."

"I know that I can too," Emily admitted. What she didn't say was that she wasn't sure that she could do this with Ryan.

Although he was one of the best at separation surgeries. It was just that part of her wanted to throttle him for not responding to her. She wasn't sure that was conducive to a good working environment.

It can be if you ignore it. He's a surgeon, you're a surgeon. He's a professional and so are you.

She shook that thought from her head. Her admiration for him, her attraction to his confidence, his charm and his devilishly handsome good looks was what had got her into this mess in the first place.

When she had been with him she hadn't felt awkward or anxious. It was like his confidence had rubbed off on her. He'd made her feel desirable.

"When will they arrive?" Emily asked.

"I've emailed you her chart and all the paperwork. I'm planning on sending them by air ambulance tomorrow, but Dr. Gary will be arriving sooner. He arrived in Portland last night, when I spoke with him about the conjoined twins. He's taking the helicopter in. He should be there soon. He's accompanying another pediatric patient with a spinal injury who arrived this morning. Thank goodness he was here."

Emily glanced at her pager. That was another patient she'd been waiting on.

Great, he was going to be working with her on that case too?

"Okay. Thanks, Ana. I'll take care of your patient. Just let me know when you think the transport with your patient will be arriving and I'll meet her."

"Will do. Thanks, Emily."

Emily disconnected the call and then groaned, burying her head in her hands.

This can't be happening.

After the debacle with Robert, when he hadn't been able to handle her promotion and her acceptance as a pediatric attending, she'd sworn she would never open her heart to a fellow surgeon again. She didn't want to deal with professional jealousy in her personal life.

It was awful.

For five years she'd managed not to date anyone. She didn't trust men. Until that conference in Vegas when Ryan had swept her off her feet. She had been a weak fool and he'd been, oh, so charming.

When Ryan hadn't responded to her messages about the baby she'd mentally kicked herself for falling into that trap again.

It had hurt to know that she'd been used like that, but she'd moved on. She wasn't going to wallow in self-pity, she had her work and this baby. She was going to make sure that she was a strong role model for her child, even if it scared her senseless to do this on her own.

Now he was on his way here and there was no hiding her pregnancy.

At least with him in Seattle she could finally get him to sign the divorce papers.

You're a professional, Emily. You've got this.

She took a deep, cleansing breath. This would be no different than dealing with the angry, pushy parents who screamed at her staff because their child's elective surgery had been canceled because a child with traumatic injuries was being rushed to the hospital.

She could deal with those people with grace, decorum and a firm hand, so she could deal with Ryan and his arrogance.

He might be a neurosurgeon, and he was one of the best in the world, but she was a more than competent pediatric surgeon, who had carried out the most successful separations of conjoined twins on the western seaboard.

She could handle Ryan for a short period of time for the sake of a patient.

Can you?

She could deal with patients and their parents because it was her job. When it came to her relationships, things went downhill fast.

Robert had often belittled her near the end of their relationship. He'd made fun of what she lacked. Differences between herself and others she'd fought hard to understand her whole life.

That moment she'd met Ryan in Vegas it had become personal and she wasn't sure she could handle him. She was afraid he'd see what she lacked.

He'd see her vulnerabilities.

Her pager went off. The air ambulance was coming in.

Her heart did a flip-flop.

Deep breath. You've got this.

Emily picked up her pager and placed it in the pocket of her white lab coat. She stood up and stretched. Her baby did a little scramble across her belly and she couldn't help but smile.

Yeah. She could do this.

She'd faced a lot worse, a lot more adversity, dealing with her mild form of high-functioning Asperger's, which meant she'd never quite fitted in. But she could handle this.

Slipping her stethoscope around her neck, she left her office and headed straight for the elevator that would take her to the helipad on top of the SMFPC.

"Teal, you're with me," she said, speaking to Dr. Amanda Teal, a surgical intern who was hovering around the nurses' station, working on her charts. "Bring a gurney and meet me on the helipad, stat."

"Of course, Dr. West." Teal ran off. The doors to the elevator dinged as they opened and Emily got on, pushing the button and code for the roof. Her nerves were shot. She stepped into the alcove and waited. It was a sunny day, and from her vantage point on the roof of Seattle Maternal Fetal Pediatric Center she could see Puget Sound clearly and the ferries on the water.

She closed her eyes and drank in the peace and quiet of a late spring morning. Then she heard the distant whirr of the helicopter and she could see the bright orange of the medical helicopter coming across the Seattle skyline.

Her heart skipped a beat.

Get a grip.

In response, she crossed her arms and bit on her bottom lip as she grounded herself to deal with facing Ryan again.

This was just about work. This was about saving lives.

Children's lives, and that was a job she took seriously. There were going to be no pleasantries. Nothing.

As the helicopter came closer, getting ready to land, she moved back to the shelter of the elevator alcove, her short blonde hair being tossed out of the neat and tidy angled bob as the wind picked up.

Dr. Teal was waiting in the alcove with a gurney.

Emily nodded to her, because it was no use talking to her over the roar of the chopper blades as the medical helicopter gently landed on the roof.

Once the helicopter had landed, the blades of the chopper began to slow and the doors of the helicopter opened.

"Come on," Emily shouted to Dr. Teal as the engines began to power down.

They ducked and ran toward the open door. The paramedics were in action, getting ready to transfer the child to her care.

As she approached the helicopter, she caught sight of Ryan and her heart did a flip-flop again. He hadn't changed much in the last six months. He was just as handsome as ever. He took her breath away. His light brown hair was perfectly tousled, those stunning blue eyes focused on the patient and paramedics. Ryan still had the scruff on his strong jaw, but it didn't hide the delectable cleft in his chin.

Get a grip.

And just as she was telling herself that, his gaze went from the patient to her. His blue eyes widened in shock, but only for a moment. It was if he was surprised to see her, like he hadn't expected her to be here, but she found that hard to believe. She looked away and moved toward the paramedic as she and Dr. Teal stepped up to take over care of the patient.

The only way she was going to survive this was to treat him like every other surgeon she dealt with, at a distance and professionally.

Which was what she should've done six months ago in Vegas, instead of letting down her guard and letting him sweep her off her feet.

Maybe because you needed that?

Emily shook that thought away.

"Patient is male, ten years old and sustained a spinal injury while riding an ATV. Patient suffered a break in his spine between C7 and T3. Dr. Gary has induced a state of medically induced coma and hypothermia," the paramedic said as they slid the stretcher out of the helicopter onto the gurney.

"Hypothermia?" Emily asked.

"To preserve the spinal cord so maybe he can walk again," Ryan said from across the stretcher as he helped load the patient onto the gurney.

Emily didn't say anything to him.

"We've got it from here," she said to the paramedic.

The paramedic nodded and handed her the chart. Emily placed it on the end of the gurney and began to wheel the patient toward the elevator. She could feel that Ryan was looking at her but she didn't care. They had to get this patient to the ICU and stabilized. The only things she wanted to discuss with Ryan was work and signing the divorce papers.

That was it.

And now was not the time to discuss the divorce.

Dr. Teal had called the elevator and the three of them got the patient's gurney onto the elevator while Emily pushed the code for the floor holding the ICU. As the doors shut, she could hear the roar of the helicopter engine come to life again. She wished that Ryan had got back on that helicopter.

Inducing hypothermia on an adult in a traumatic spinal injury often had a good outcome, but a pediatric patient? It was frowned upon.

What was Ryan thinking? Was he this arrogant that he believed he was God or something?

"What the heck were you thinking, inducing therapeutic hypothermia in a pediatric patient?" Emily berated. She was so angry, but it really wasn't about his method of treatment. She wanted to scream at him for ignoring her for the last six months.

For not responding about the baby.

For hurting her. But she couldn't say those things in front of Dr. Teal so she attacked him over his treatment choice to blow off the anger she felt in that moment of seeing him again.

Dr. Teal's eyes widened and for one moment Emily felt bad for exploding in front of her intern, but it was only for a moment, because when she looked across the gurney at Ryan he was smiling. That charming, arrogant smile that had got her into trouble in the first place.

"It's good to see you too, wife."

CHAPTER TWO

WHY DID HE have to be so cocky?

The moment he said the word, he was sure that fire was going to come shooting out of Emily's nostrils and he really understood the meaning of that old saying, *If looks could kill*, from the way she was glaring at him. But, dammit, she looked just as good as ever.

Her blonde, almost platinum-colored, hair was shorter, but it suited her and he couldn't help but remember the way that if he kissed her just below her earlobe it made her sigh in pleasure. He'd been a fool to walk away from her.

You weren't the only one who walked away, remember?

When he'd woken up in that Las Vegas hotel room, he had been alone and the only thing left of her had been the marriage certificate on the night stand.

He'd tried to reach out to her but she hadn't responded, and by the time she'd reached out to him, he'd been boarding a plane heading to the Middle East.

And Emily had never reached out to him again until he'd received the divorce papers a week ago. That was the first he'd heard from her. It had been around the same time that Dr. Ruchi had asked him to consult on the conjoined twins case.

He'd figured it would be nice to hand deliver the divorce papers to her and put an end to that reckless night in Las Vegas, and also lay her ghost rest, because for the last six months she'd been all he could think about.

The fact that another woman haunted him so much scared him, because he remembered the last time that had happened.

He'd thought Morgan had loved him. She'd fallen pregnant and, without telling him, she'd terminated the pregnancy and left.

He never wanted to get involved with another woman again. Not in a serious relationship anyway. One-night stands were fine, but marriage?

What had he been thinking?

It was a relief that Emily seemed to want the same thing.

He had mentally prepared himself for the worst by coming to Seattle and facing his demons, but he hadn't been prepared to really see her again, because when he'd first seen Emily in Vegas he'd been a lost man. She had been gorgeous and though she'd been a bit shy, there had been something about her that had made him want to know her better.

He'd fallen for her intelligence, her beauty, her charm, her lack of dancing skills, but, just like every other woman, she'd used him and she'd left.

He'd become used to leaving first. He wasn't used to it being the other way around. It suited him, though, because he'd been unable to deal with that heartache Morgan had inflicted on him.

Emily opened her mouth to say something else and

then glanced over her shoulder at the intern, who was at the end of the gurney, and thought better of it.

The doors to the elevator opened and they wheeled the gurney toward an open room in the ICU where they could get his patient settled and Ryan could reverse the hypothermia and get busy repairing this young boy's spine.

"Dr. Teal, would you get Dr. Gary some scrubs and a surgical cap?" Emily asked as they made sure the patient was stabilized.

"Of course, Dr. West." The intern left the ICU room and the team of ICU nurses took over as Emily picked up the patient's chart and motioned him to follow her. She set the chart down at the nurses' station and turned to face him, her arms crossed, and it was then he noticed the round swell under her scrubs.

His heart skipped a beat. He couldn't believe what he was seeing. She was pregnant and she hadn't told him? Just seeing her like that caused a flashback.

"You could've told me you were pregnant!" Ryan shouted as Morgan packed up her belongings.

"Why? We're not married and I don't want to be a mother. My career is my focus now."

"I have a right to know!"

"You do. I just told you, but it's done. Now we can both move on."

He shook that memory away. He hadn't wanted to be a father, but by the time he'd come back to New York after a business trip Morgan had already terminated the pregnancy and the relationship.

He'd been kept in the dark.

Apparently, history was repeating itself.

And he was scared by the prospect. He just had to handle this delicately.

"You look good, Emily."

"Don't," she said, shaking her head.

"What?"

"You know what." She looked toward the ICU pod. "That is a pediatric patient."

"With a traumatic spinal cord injury," he answered, confused. "I did what was best for transfer from Portland."

Emily bit her bottom lip and shook her head. "Therapeutic hypothermia is not tolerated well in pediatric patients."

"The boy is ten," Ryan snapped. "He's not an infant and I put him in a medicated coma. He's old enough to tolerate it for a short time and he's young enough to bounce back. There won't be significant loss in brain function that he can't recover with extensive physiotherapy, which he was going to need if I left him a quadriplegic."

She sighed and her expression softened. "I assume you got the parents' permission."

"This is not my first time performing this on a preteen pediatric spinal cord injury. We'll reverse the hypothermia and I'll repair the spine," he snapped, annoyed she was questioning him. And he realized this argument had nothing to do with his treatment plan of the patient and everything to do with the pregnancy and divorce papers.

She was angry.

Well, he was angry too.

"Is it mine?" he asked, catching her off guard.

"Yes." She blushed, the pink creeping her way up into her high cheekbones. "So, you did get my emails?"

Ryan cocked an eyebrow. "What emails?"

"I sent you an email when I found out I was pregnant and then several others. There was no response so I assumed you didn't want anything to do with me and the baby."

"You assumed?"

"You didn't answer me," she hissed.

"I didn't get the emails, Emily. I didn't know that you were pregnant."

Emily was going to say something further when Dr. Teal returned with scrubs.

"I have the surgical scrubs, Dr. West."

"Thanks," Ryan said, taking them from the intern. "Can you prep an operating room for me?"

"Of course, Dr. Gary." Dr. Teal left and Emily glared at him.

"She's a surgical intern. She's here to learn under my guidance today."

"And isn't it her job to prep the operating room? It was when I was a surgical intern," Ryan said.

Emily's eyes narrowed. "You'll want a resident. Dr. Sharipova is one of the best and most promising pediatric surgical residents. He's been an invaluable asset to me."

"Thank you. I'm sure he'll be great help, but I would also like you in there. I was told that you would be in the operating room with me on this and I told the patients' parents that the best pediatric surgeon on the western seaboard would be assisting me in the operating room."

"Of course I'll be in there."

"Good." There was more that he wanted to say to her, but he didn't want to say it in the middle of the ICU with patients and other staff members around them. This was not the place to talk about their baby or their marriage.

Of course, after calling her his wife in front of her surgical intern that secret was going to spread around the hospital like wildfire.

"Can you show me a place I can get changed into my scrubs and possibly store my stuff? All my luggage is being shipped to my rental in Seattle, so I don't have a bag or much with me."

Her expression softened again. "Sure, I'll show you where the attendings' lounge is. Follow me."

Emily could feel all the eyes on her as she and Ryan left the ICU. She was pretty sure that most of the staff by now knew what he'd called her. Not that she could blame Dr. Teal for saying something. It was pretty shocking and she felt bad that Amanda had been mixed up in that tense moment.

She was feeling bad for calling Ryan out and for putting Amanda into the middle of all those emotions she was feeling.

Although she'd never used therapeutic hypothermia on a patient, she shouldn't have questioned his tactics. He was a brilliant surgeon. Her reaction was not keeping her emotions out of the mix. If anything, it was causing more problems.

Her plan had been to treat Ryan like any colleague and it was rare that she called out another practitioner on their methods in public like that. Especially when neurosurgery was not her specialty. And especially since it wasn't even about that. She was angry he'd never responded to her and then he'd made her look like a fool in front of Dr. Teal. She'd hated it when Robert had done that to her.

Usually she was calm, cool and collected. She prided herself on professional behavior. Behavior she'd worked so hard to learn. What she'd just pulled was not her usual behavior and she was annoyed with herself for letting her emotions get the better of her.

The attendings' lounge was, mercifully, empty.

"There's an empty cubby over there." She pointed to the one that was furthest from the door but she stayed close to the door, because it was an escape route.

"Thanks." Ryan walked over to the cubby, slipped off his leather jacket and placed it inside. "I did get one message, by the way."

That shocked her. "Oh?"

"The divorce papers."

"But not news of my pregnancy. I sent you ten emails."

"I told you the night we got married that I had to catch a flight. I was overseas and in an area where internet connection was spotty. I wasn't trying to ignore you."

He was unbuttoning his shirt to put on his scrubs and Emily tried not to watch. She wanted to believe him.

"I'd had a lot to drink that night. I don't remember you telling me that."

"I remember, sort of. I guess we' both had a lot to drink that night because an Elvis impersonator married us? Really? That sounds tacky." It was a joke meant to break the tension and it did.

A smile tugged at the corners of her lips and she couldn't help but laugh just a little. "Right. Completely tacky."

"I'm glad you decided to keep the baby," he said softly.

"Of course I would."

A strange expression crossed his face as he slipped off his shirt and then pulled his scrub top over his head. For a moment Emily thought that he didn't quite believe that she would've kept this baby. Everyone had a choice, but she knew she'd wanted this child the moment the stick had turned blue.

Was it planned? No, but she was happy to be pregnant. She liked kids, which was why she'd become a pediatric surgeon.

"After this surgery we really need to sit down and talk," he said.

"Right. About the conjoined twins. I have to go over the chart…"

He cocked an eyebrow. "What're you talking about?"

"The conjoined twins case. What're you talking about?"

"I'm talking about our marriage and the baby."

Her heart skipped a beat and she could feel the warmth creeping up her necks into her cheeks. "Ryan, we don't have a marriage."

"We're still married. We can't get an annulment and I'm not sure about signing the divorce papers."

Of course.

He had to make this difficult by not signing the papers. It was frustrating.

"Is that what you want to talk about? You want to talk about the divorce? It's all laid out in the papers."

"No, I don't want to talk about a divorce, Emily," he said in frustration. "I want to talk about you and me and the baby. About what we should do."

She couldn't help but laugh at that. "There is no you and I, Ryan. We made a silly mistake in Vegas."

"I don't think it was silly," he said seriously.

"What? You can't be serious."

"I am serious, Emily. I want to raise our baby…" He paused and looked a bit uncertain. "I want us to raise our baby together."

CHAPTER THREE

EMILY DIDN'T WANT to talk about it. She thought the whole idea was absurd. He wanted to talk about their relationship? He wanted to make it work? To raise a baby together? They didn't have a relationship. They'd met, had a few drinks and had a one-night stand. And she wasn't even sure she totally believed him about not getting her emails.

He'd acted surprised, though.

Although Robert had been a good actor too. She'd been duped before. Emily bit her lip. She wasn't sure what to think.

Other than the work he'd published and the talks she'd listened to, she knew nothing about him and he knew nothing about her. That was not the basis for any kind of relationship. Her parents were best friends. They'd taken their time to get to know each other and they'd had a long, happy marriage.

They still had a good marriage.

Ryan and she didn't have that.

They'd had one night together. That was the basis for nothing.

There was a tiny kick and she looked down at her belly. Well, maybe it wasn't completely nothing, but still she didn't want to talk about this with Ryan. They didn't have a real marriage. Why did he seem so keen to get involved now?

"We're not talking about this," she said quickly. "I'll meet you down in the OR."

"I don't know where the OR floor is and I don't have access to it."

Dammit.

"Finished getting dressed," she said through pursed lips.

"Emily—"

"No," she snapped. "The only thing we're going to talk about after this surgery is the conjoined twin case. It's a very important case and the mother is arriving tomorrow. If the babies survive the birth and make it through their first week of life, we have to talk about a plan to do the separation. That's all I want to talk about right now. Just patients, just cases. That's it, Ryan. That's all I can handle." And it was true. She was feeling overwhelmed. She hadn't felt this way since Robert had betrayed her and she hated this feeling.

His eyes narrowed and he undid the buckle to his jeans. "Fine."

Only she had a feeling by the way he'd said "Fine" that this wasn't over and that this discussion was going to continue. He was persistent enough. It was something she'd admired about him. He was driven and that's why he was the best there was in neurosurgery and why she'd striven to continue to rise in her chosen field.

There had been so many people who'd said she couldn't be a surgeon when she struggled with Asperger's, when she struggled with social anxieties, but she had risen above so much to get where she was. She worked longer hours. She worked hard.

To be perfect. To be the best.

Her pregnancy made her human and that had been a hard pill to swallow, but she'd never shied away from her mistakes, but to think that she and Ryan had something more than just a momentary attraction was silly.

It's not momentary. You're still attracted to him.

And her cheeks heated as he picked up the scrub pants. She cleared her throat and looked away. "I'll be out in the hall and then we can head down to the OR."

"Fine," he said, but there was a devilish twinkle in his eyes as if he knew that he was affecting her and she hated that.

She slipped out of the attendings' lounge and leaned against the wall, closing her eyes and trying to catch her breath. When she opened them again, she could see a few of the interns, nurses and even physicians watching her, whispering as they looked at her belly.

Dammit.

She hated being the center of attention when it came to gossip. She didn't mind it when it was about her work, but when it involved her baby and now her supposed marriage to Ryan, it bothered her.

The door to the lounge opened up and Ryan stepped out wearing scrubs instead of his street clothes. He looked good in the dark blue of the SMFPC attending colors. The color brought out the intensity of his cerulean eyes.

"You okay?" he asked.

"Fine."

Liar.

"You look a bit pale. Are you overdoing it?"

"No. I'm fine. Let's go, they're waiting for us in OR two and I don't want that patient in therapeutic hypothermia any longer than he has to be."

"Lead the way."

Emily led Ryan down to the OR floor. They didn't say anything to each other, but she could feel the stares as they passed through the halls. Gossip spread like wildfire in this hospital and she would have to have a word with Dr. Teal.

They stopped just outside the wide hall that led toward the many operating rooms. She pulled on her scrub cap and showed Ryan where to get a generic one. She hung up her white lab coat, changed her shoes. Ryan covered his shoes with booties. He'd have a pair of sneakers that would be just for the OR floor.

"You ready?" she asked.

"Always." He smiled at her and it was full of confidence.

"Come on." She punched in a code and opened the door. She always liked this walk down the hallway. It was calming. There were gurneys and equipment waiting in the wings, sometimes there would be a gurney roll by that was accompanied by a parent and a child life support person as SMFPC supported the parental presence at induction, and those cases always made her smile.

There was fear in the parents' eyes, hidden behind their masks, but they were strong for their children and their presence really promoted the well-being and health of the children.

Then there were cases like this little boy they were attending.

Priority A, where a young life was on the line.

She ran a hand over her belly and glanced up at Ryan,

whose gaze was on her belly, before he met her eyes briefly. There was pain in his eyes, but also fear.

"The scrub room is here," she said, breaking the tension that fell between them.

He nodded and walked into the room before her. The scrub room overlooked the operating room where their young patient was lying. The rest of the operating room team was prepping him and the anesthesiologists were waiting.

Ryan was scrubbing, staring at his patient intently, as she often did herself. She would play out the surgery in her mind, like a playbook.

"Do you think you'll be successful?" she asked, because she knew he was a great neurosurgeon but she'd never worked with him before and none of the neurosurgeons at SMFPC would ever attempt therapeutic hypothermia on a child younger than sixteen. Ryan was a bit of a maverick. Maybe that's why she'd been so attracted to him in the first place. He was so different from Robert, who had always done things by the book.

So different from her.

"Of course." He smiled confidently. "I've done this before."

"Good, because I've never done this."

"You've never done a spinal decompression and a repair of a fracture?"

"Yes. I've assisted with that, but I've never dealt with a child in hypothermia like this."

"It'll work, Emily," Ryan said gently, before he shook off his hands and toweled them dry. "Trust me."

Emily continued scrubbing as he headed into the operating room. He'd asked her to trust him and she wanted to do that, for their patient's sake, but she had a hard time trusting someone she didn't know.

She liked routine. She liked certain anesthesiologists, certain residents, certain scrub nurses in her operating room. The routine gave her a sense of calm, and she'd never worked with Ryan before.

He's the best.

And that's what she had to keep telling herself. She shook off her hands and then headed into the operating room. Her favorite scrub nurse, Nancy, helped her into her gown and gloves. Emily also had to remind herself that she was not lead surgeon here.

Ryan was.

She might be the head of pediatric surgery, but he was the neurosurgeon and she had to put her faith in him and what he thought was best. He'd been there when the accident had come in. He'd got all the permissions from the patient's parents. He knew the chart best.

Emily looked up into the gallery and could see the chief of surgery watching, as well as a few of the interns and residents.

They'd come to see the show.

Ryan's reputation preceded him.

She had to get a grip on all her self-doubt and focus on this moment, because soon there would be a set of babies on this table and it would be a team, led by her and Ryan, as they worked to separate the babies and give them a chance at life.

She approached the operating table and took the second position across from him. Dr. Sharipova was there, as well as Dr. Teal, but Dr. Teal would just be observing.

"Dr. Teal, would you read off the chart for the record?" Ryan said, totally ignoring the fact Dr. Sharipova was the resident and should be reading it out for the OR record.

Dr. Teal looked toward her and Emily nodded. "Go on, Dr. Teal."

Amanda nodded. "Jason Klassen is a ten-year-old male patient with a break in the spine from the C7 to the T3. Patient was placed in a medicated coma and induced into therapeutic hypothermia in Portland for transfer. This surgery will reverse the hypothermia and we will attempt to repair the damage to the spine."

"Not attempt, Dr. Teal," Ryan said brightly. "We will."

"Right," Dr. Teal responded, her voice catching.

"Ready when you are, Dr. Gary," Emily said.

Ryan nodded. "Scalpel."

Emily might not want to admit that she was tired and hurting after hours in the operating room, but Ryan could tell that she was.

She was sitting on a bench just outside the OR and was hunched over. Her head was propped up by one arm and her eyes were closed. He could tell by the way her shoulders moved that she was taking deep breaths.

It had been a long surgery, but it had been successful. The tests on the nerves showed function in the patient's legs. It was just a matter of time before they could bring him out of the coma and see what damage had been done to his brain, but Ryan didn't believe that there would be any damage. Therapeutic hypothermia worked.

Right now, that wasn't his concern. He was worried that Emily was pushing herself too hard and that she was putting herself and the baby in jeopardy.

He straddled the bench beside her. It took all his willpower not to reach out and touch her, but he thought the gesture would not be a welcome one. In fact, the moment he'd arrived he'd had the distinct feeling that his presence here was unwelcome.

And he aimed to change that. He'd give her the support she needed while he was here. He owed her that much. He was terrified about being a father and he wasn't sure he knew how to be a good one.

His own father had abandoned him and his mother instead of ranching on his mother's family's land. He knew nothing about being there for a kid. He wasn't sure he could.

Morgan never gave you the chance to decide.

Maybe that was for the best. His life was too transient. He liked it that way.

Do you?

He shook his head.

He was a fool.

"You okay?"

"Fine." She sat up straight, but he could see that she was exhausted.

"It's a long time on your feet."

"I'm aware of that."

"When did you eat last?" he asked.

Emily shook her head. "Lunch, just before I got the call from Dr. Ruchi about the conjoined twins and before you decided to grace me with your presence."

He chuckled. "Come on, let's get something to eat."

"There's no time. The patient's parents have arrived and are in the waiting room. I think we have to go talk to them and take them to their son."

"We can go talk to them, but one of the interns can take them to their son in the ICU. After we talk to them, you're getting something to eat. Doctor's orders."

Emily sighed and stood up. "Fine."

"You're not going to argue with me?" he teased.

"No, because you're right and I'm starving. Let's go talk to the Klassens. Dr. Teal can take them up to see their son." Emily stood up, but she closed her eyes and the blood drained from her face.

Ryan reached out and held her steady. "Whoa, you're definitely not fine."

"Just a bit dizzy. Okay, you're right. Today I pushed it too far. I haven't been present in a pediatric orthopedic or neurosurgery since I got pregnant."

He helped her sit back down. "I want you to stay here. I'll go speak with the parents and then I'll be right back."

She nodded. "Okay."

"I'll be right back. Don't move."

"I won't."

He didn't want to leave her, but he had a duty to his patient's parents. They were probably sick with worry. He took Dr. Teal with him so that the young intern could take Jason's parents to the ICU, and because Dr. Teal was with him it didn't take him long to find the waiting area.

He explained to Jason's parents the procedure and the outcome. Jason's family would be in Seattle for some time while Jason went through extensive physiotherapy after he healed.

At least with kids they bounced back.

After Dr. Teal had taken Jason's parents up to the ICU, Ryan turned round and went back to the operating room floor, using Emily's pass.

She'd stayed where he'd left her.

Only she was sitting on the floor, her back to the wall

and her head between her knees. He rushed over to her and knelt down.

"Emily?"

"I really need to get something to eat." A weak smile tugged at her lips and he couldn't help but smile at her.

"Come on. I'll take you to the nicest place in town."

"Don't you have to stay while your patient is in the ICU?" she asked as he helped her to her feet.

"I do, but the nicest place in town isn't far."

She laughed. "I hate to disappoint you, the cafeteria is not the nicest place in town."

"Well, it will have to do until I can take you to the nicest place in town. Where is that, by the way?"

She chuckled again and shrugged as they began to walk slowly away from the OR. "I don't know. I've been in Seattle for five years but I haven't got out and done much."

"You're not from Seattle?" he asked.

"No, I'm from Salt Lake City and, no, before you ask, I'm not Mormon. My parents are, but I never connected with the religion or any religion, just science."

Ryan nodded. He understood that. Science had exerted the same sort of pull on him. His mother had wanted him to farm her family's land, but by the time he'd hit eighteen it had been apparent that he was not suited to a life of ranching. That was about the time his mother had stopped talking to him and when he'd learned to fend for himself.

"Well, asking about your religious affiliation was the furthest thing from my mind."

"Sorry, it's just when I tell people where I'm from, that's the first thing I'm asked." She glanced up at him. "Sorry I'm walking so slowly."

"It's fine. Take your time." He couldn't help but wonder why she was apologizing so much.

"It's frustrating," she admitted. "I would spend my time racing around this hospital. I could get from the ICU to the emergency room in five minutes and now I'm significantly slower."

He felt like he should apologize, but he hadn't been the only willing party the night they'd conceived their child. What he did feel bad about was missing the first six months of her pregnancy, for her doing this on her own.

He was ashamed about that and angry at himself. He might not be sure about being a father, but he'd never meant to leave her alone. If he'd only known…

"Let's get you something to eat."

They walked into the cafeteria and Emily sat down. Ryan went to the counter and grabbed a couple of sandwiches and some water. He brought it back to her and sat down next to her.

"Thanks for this," Emily said. "They really do make good sandwiches."

"Still, there's probably somewhere better and I'm going to have to find it and take you to it."

She raised her eyebrows. "Why?"

"Emily, we have a lot to talk about."

"Other than work, we don't. I meant what I said in those messages, I can raise this baby on my own. We both made a mistake—"

"I don't walk away from my responsibilities." He was annoyed that she was giving him an out. He didn't want an out. Well, he did, but he didn't either. Right now, he wasn't sure what he wanted. But he was here now.

The last time that had happened, he'd lost a child

and it had hurt. He was going to take responsibility for this one.

There wasn't any way he was going to walk away. He was going to help Emily for as long as he could.

CHAPTER FOUR

EMILY SAT AT a desk in a quiet part of the ICU. Her shift was almost over, but she didn't want to go home just yet. Not that there was anything to go home to and she felt bad for trying to push Ryan away. It's just that she'd never been able to rely on anyone other than her parents She'd got to where she was by working hard to overcome what her teachers had told her would hold her back. The only time she'd foolishly relied on someone else had been when she was with Robert.

He'd belittled her and cheated on her.

Why would it be any different with Ryan?

So she'd given him an out.

And he seemed to want it but said that he didn't.

He'd been so mad when she'd suggested that he didn't need to be involved in his child's life. They'd eaten their sandwiches in silence, until he'd got an urgent page about Jason and left to go to the ICU.

Emily had finished the rest of her meal and then made her way back up to the ICU floor to do the last rounds on her patients before one of her residents took over to cover the night shift. Now she looked up from her charting to see Ryan by Jason's bed and he was recording information into a computer.

Ryan might move from hospital to hospital and never hold down a steady position, but he was passionate and caring when it came to his patients. Dr. Ruchi believed in him and wanted him to be the neurosurgeon on the conjoined twin case.

Emily turned back to her computer and pulled up the chart information that Dr. Ruchi had sent over. She opened the MRI scan to take a look at the babies. There was a good chance that these babies could be successfully separated. They shared a liver and part of the colon and there were three kidneys, which meant one twin would only get one kidney, but they had four legs, four arms and two sets of genitals. It was a matter of trying to separate the liver and colon. And then there was the spine and the nerves that controlled the legs.

The babies were partially back to back.

Where they were joined it would be hard to separate them without paralyzing them. She scrubbed a hand over her face.

You've done other separations. This is no different.

And all those conjoined cases had been successful. The key to success was gathering a strong team and discussing the plan of attack.

Now, if only Ryan would discuss the plans with her, instead of insisting on talking about their baby, who was healthy and fine.

She closed the files and logged off the computer. She finished her charting and handed them to the nurse in charge. Emily knew that the resident in charge would know what to do. She wouldn't have to talk to them.

With one last look at Ryan, still by Jason's bedside, she headed to the attendings' lounge so that she could change before she headed for home. She needed rest if she was going to be ready to face the mother of the conjoined twins tomorrow with the OB/GYN assigned to deliver the babies.

That was the first step, settling the mother into the hospital, before, in a few weeks, once the babies were bigger and stronger, safely delivering them by C-section and hoping they survived long enough to consider doing the separation surgery.

She quickly changed and was just pulling on her coat when Ryan came into the lounge.

"There you are," he said.

"I'm going home," she answered, without looking at him. "I'm tired and I need rest before our patient arrives tomorrow."

"Good." He rubbed the back of his neck. "I'm sorry for snapping at you."

"It's fine. It's a lot. I get it." Emily wrapped her scarf around her neck. "Try and get some sleep and we'll talk tomorrow."

"How about we talk tonight?"

"About what, Ryan? Our baby, or what I wanted to talk about?"

"The conjoined twins case. It's only seven and the resident on duty has my pager number. Why don't we go and have a real meal? A sandwich is a pretty poor meal."

Say no. Just go home.

"Fine. There's a little bistro not far from here. That way, if you're paged you can get back fairly fast and not get lost."

"Sounds good."

Emily nodded and stepped out of the lounge. It didn't take him long before he was dressed. They walked in silence together out of the hospital. It was a cool night. It was the tail end of spring and soon it would be summer.

It was her favorite season.

She was not a fan of winter.

"It's just over there," Emily said, pointing to the small bistro on the corner just across the street from the hospital. "It's a favorite haunt of the chief of surgery in the morning. So if you're ever looking to have some one-on-one time to schmooze with him, this is the place he'll be."

Ryan chuckled. "Noted. Although I don't have to schmooze. People are usually the ones schmoozing me."

Emily laughed.

"What?" Ryan asked.

"Oh, just…you know when you say a word over and over again it sounds funny, like it's lost all meaning."

Ryan cocked an eyebrow and looked at her like she'd lost her mind, and maybe she had. She was tired and she was getting a bit silly from exhaustion.

"I can't say that I've noticed that."

"Say schmooze a few more times," she teased. She had a sense of déjà vu and then she remembered the mojito talk during their wedding. She couldn't help but smile.

"I think not." He opened the door to the small bistro.

"Is it just the two of you tonight?" the maître d' asked.

"Yes," Ryan said.

"This way." He lead them to the back to a corner booth that was tucked away and quiet. Emily slid in and the maître d' set down a couple of menus. "Your waiter will be with you shortly."

"Thank you," Emily said, as she picked up the menu.

Ryan glanced at the menu briefly, but he didn't look

particularly interested in the food. "So, you wanted to talk about our patient."

"I do. I like to be prepared."

"Hi, my name is Dennis and I'll be your waiter tonight. Can I bring you anything?" the waiter asked, interrupting.

Ryan didn't even look at him. "I'll have an espresso."

"Water for me," Emily said.

Dennis nodded and left.

"How do you know Ana Ruchi?" Emily asked.

"She's not our patient," Ryan teased.

Emily rolled her eyes. "I am aware, but Dr. Ruchi was my mentor when I was a surgical resident and trying to decide my path. She encouraged me to move into pediatric surgery and I was wondering how a neurosurgeon such as yourself knew her. I mean, you know I'm from Salt Lake City, but I don't know anything about you."

A devilish smile played at the corners of his lips, lips that she suddenly and vividly remembered kissing her. "You know a lot more about me than most."

Heat bloomed in her cheeks. "That's not what I'm talking about, Ryan."

He sighed. "Fine, you want to know how I know Dr. Ruchi. I'm the one who removed a substantial aneurysm from her brain about a year ago."

Emily's stomach twisted in a knot. Ana had never told her anything about that. An aneurysm? She hadn't even known that Ana had had surgery. Had she missed some cue that would have told her Ana was having a hard time? "What? When?"

"A year ago, just before we met, actually. She came to me when the aneurysm was threatening her eyesight and thus threatening her ability to care for her patients, and she had me clip it."

"You shouldn't be telling me this! Doctor-patient confidentiality."

Ryan grinned and leaned forward. "Ana knew that you would question my connection to her and gave me the okay to tell you."

Ana knew her so well.

Emily bit her lip and cursed under her breath. She was going to have several words with Ana about keeping that little bit of information from her.

You didn't tell Ana that Ryan was the father of your baby.

"So that's why Ana trusts you to assist with the separation of the conjoined twins."

"I have also done several separations of twins, especially where the nerves and spinal cord are involved. I have looked at the file, Emily. I know, approximately, how many nerves are shared between the two girls. I know that this separation will be tricky and that we have to prep for it, but it's not like we're doing the surgery tomorrow. Those babies need to be delivered and then they need to be stable. And then they have to be older than a week before we can even attempt the surgery."

Emily was impressed, just as impressed as she had been when she'd first heard him speak at that conference in Las Vegas. She'd forgotten this side of him and how impressive he truly was.

This is the kind of thinking that got us into trouble the last time. Remember?

She had been dazzled by him and an innocent meeting for drinks had turned into several drinks for both of them and then a trip to that shady wedding chapel on the wrong side of Vegas. It had also led to a night of passion. One that she'd tried hard to forget but couldn't.

The waiter brought their drinks. "Are we ready to order?"

"I need a few minutes," Emily said, clearing her throat. "I'm sorry."

"No worries. I'll give you both a few minutes." The waiter left.

"I think I should figure out what I'm going to have for when he comes back." She picked up her menu and decided on a salad. "Are you going to have something to eat?"

Ryan shook his head. "I might have another espresso, but that sandwich was good enough. I'll have something later, but I want to stay awake to be with Jason tonight. I'm hoping we'll be able to bring him out of a medicated coma in a couple of days."

"And you think it'll work?"

Ryan nodded and smiled. "You asked me that before."

She groaned. "I did, didn't I?"

"It's okay, Emily. It's been a very… I don't even have the words. It's been a very interesting day."

"It has." She took a sip of her water. "So, you saved my mentor's life?"

"I did."

"Now, why don't you tell me where you're from?"

A strange expression crossed his face. "Why?"

"I told you where I'm from."

"And you think that knowing where I come from will help you figure me out?" he asked.

"I think so. I'd like to know the place you call home since you don't have a practice set up or a hospital that you call home."

He pursed his lips and his expression hardened as

he fiddled with his espresso cup. "I did, but it didn't work out."

"You had a practice?"

"Yes," he said tightly, and she realized she had touched a nerve. She couldn't help but wonder what had happened. "Briefly, in New York City, but it still required a lot of travel."

"So…"

"I'm from Wyoming. A small town and, yes, mostly Mormons there too, but my mother wasn't."

She blushed again. "Thanks?"

"Well, you announced your religion or lack of it to me."

She laughed. "So I did."

"Anything else you want to know?"

"Schooling. You're from Wyoming, so where did you attend medical school?"

"Harvard."

"Impressive."

He shrugged. "Not as impressive as you. You're one of the best pediatric surgeons on the western seaboard, but you don't brag about that."

Emily blushed. "Why brag?"

"Why not?"

The question made her feel uncomfortable. There was nothing to brag about. Diligent studying and hard work had got her here.

"How do you know that I'm considered one of the top pediatric surgeons?"

"I did my research about you after I woke up and all that was left of you was a marriage certificate with your name on it." He took another sip of coffee. "Your name and Elvis's real name, which, by the way, is George Luongo."

Emily laughed at that and shook her head.

"Are you ready to order?" the waiter asked.

"Yes, I'll have your house salad with chicken and he'll have another espresso." Emily handed the waiter the menus.

"I'll be back shortly." The waiter left.

"So, you looked me up online?" Emily asked.

"Don't tell me you didn't look me up too?" he asked.

"I did, to find out where to get the message to you that I was pregnant. I had read your published papers before the conference. Still, I had no idea that you studied at Harvard and that you were from Wyoming."

Ryan shrugged. "It doesn't matter where I'm from."

"I think it matters. Where you're from says a lot about you. Family and places shape us."

That strange, pained expression crossed his face again. "I have to disagree with that."

"Why?"

He scrubbed a hand over his face. "Let's talk about the case, why don't we? I assume that you'll want to run through simulations of it."

"I will. I do so every time I do a separation of conjoined twins."

"Have you ever lost one?" he asked.

The question was dark and caught her off guard. She didn't like to think about the patients she'd lost, because there were always patients she lost. They were always there, in the back of her mind, and they shaped what she did the next time.

They helped her fight harder.

To save more lives, but she didn't want to dwell on them.

"No, I actually haven't lost a set of conjoined twins and I don't plan to start."

He smiled. "I'm glad, and the same with me."

The waiter brought her food and his second cup of expresso. They didn't say much as she ate some of her salad and he finished his drink.

She was feeling better about Dr. Ruchi's choice of neurosurgeon to help her. And they had worked well in surgery today on Jason's spine. It was always tricky when working with a surgeon for the first time.

You were never sure if your styles would mesh. And Emily had always been particular about the way she ran her operating room. She had been worried when she'd let Ryan take the helm, but after a few minutes of being his assistant on Jason's surgery, she had seen that all those worries had been unfounded.

They'd worked well together and she knew that they would work well together on the conjoined twins case, if they could get over all their personal issues.

There was an ear-piercing scream which made the hair on the back of her neck stand on end. Ryan leapt to his feet and Emily stood up. They could see a woman on the floor of the bistro, trying to hold her small child as the child was having what looked like a seizure.

Ryan ran over to the woman and Emily followed him.

"Help!" the mother cried as she tried to hold her child. "I don't know what happened!"

"Has your child had a seizure before?" Emily asked as she peeled off her jacket and folded it, slipping it under the little girl's head as Ryan helped roll the child on her side.

"No. She was fine and then she just started staring off into space before she collapsed. Are you doctors?" the frantic mother asked.

"Yes," Ryan said.

Emily watched the little girl go through the shaking, the rigid muscles of the seizure and timed it. She'd seen these types of seizure before, but if someone was unfamiliar with them, they could be scared by them. Tonic clonic seizures were scary.

"Her lips are blue! She's not breathing." The mother tried to reach for her child, but Ryan held her back.

"It's okay," Emily said calmly. "She's having a tonic clonic seizure. She has stopped breathing and it's super-scary, but it's only for a moment."

It was a matter of seconds before the little girl began to breathe again and her movements began to lessen, and as the seizure ended Emily could hear the distant wail of an ambulance approaching. The little girl wasn't responding and Emily frowned.

That wasn't a good sign. Emily reached down and unbuttoned the child's shirt as the paramedics came into the bistro with their stretcher.

Ryan stood up and began to tell the paramedics what had happened.

"Where are you planning on taking her?" Emily asked the paramedic.

"Seattle General," the paramedic answered.

"No, you're not taking her there. You're taking her across the road to SMFPC. I'm the head of pediatric surgery and Dr. Gary here is a neurosurgeon. This is our patient," Emily said firmly.

The paramedic nodded and Ryan helped her to her feet.

"You're supposed to go home and rest," Ryan whispered.

Emily shrugged. "This is my patient who just had her

first seizure, according to her mother. I'm going to need a neurosurgeon to help me."

"Fine, but once we have this patient settled I'm going to make sure that you get home and rest." Ryan left then to pay the bill, while Emily checked on her young patient, who was just starting to come to.

She picked up her jacket off the floor.

"What happened?" the little girl asked.

"You had a seizure," Emily said.

"Who are you?" the girl asked, confused. Her voice sounded a bit slurred, which was also not a good sign.

"A doctor. You're going to come to my hospital and I'm going to check out everything before I can let your mom take you home. Is that okay?"

The little girl nodded.

"Thank you," the mother said. "I'm so glad you were here."

Emily nodded. "We'll take good care of her. Dr. Gary and I will see you in a few moments."

The mother nodded and followed the paramedics out of the bistro.

Emily sighed and rubbed her belly. Her baby was going crazy, her feet ached and there was a part of her that wished she could have a strong espresso too.

You can power through this.

"You ready?" Ryan asked as he slipped on his coat.

Emily nodded. "Let's go."

She'd get to sleep eventually, because she was more than ready to put this emotional, long, drawn-out day to bed.

CHAPTER FIVE

RYAN HAD BEEN up for hours. Usually it didn't bother him, but it had taken him a while to travel from San Diego to Portland to Seattle and he was exhausted. Jason had been stable the last time he'd checked on him in the ICU.

Now his concern was Raquel, the little girl who'd had the tonic clonic seizure in the bistro the previous night. Ryan glanced at the clock. It was one in the morning and he hoped that Emily had made her way back to her home and bed. She needed rest.

Ryan took another sip of his now cold coffee as he waited for the MRI images of Raquel to come up.

There had been no history of epilepsy, but he wasn't going to rule that out just yet. Still, something bothered him about her seizure. It was the length that it had lasted and the fact it had taken the girl a long time to regain consciousness.

Emily had timed the seizure and it had lasted for more than five minutes.

Please, don't be a tumor. Please, don't be a tumor.

The coffee tasted bitter and he wished he could warm it up, but he wasn't going to leave the MRI room until he had the image.

"The image is loading now, Dr. Gary."

Ryan leaned over the technician as the scan loaded. And the moment it loaded, Ryan's heart sank as he saw exactly what he didn't want to see.

Dammit.

"Can you send those to my email?" Ryan asked the technician.

"Of course, Dr. Gary."

Ryan nodded and left the MRI lab, letting the nurse take care of Raquel. He wanted to talk to Emily before he talked to Raquel's mother. Raquel was already under observation, so he would talk to them in the morning. He had to formulate his next steps.

Yes, there was a growth in the little girl's brain, but that didn't mean that it was malignant. It could be benign. He had to get a biopsy of the growth and that would determine whether he attempted surgery, or if it was even possible.

This was the worst part of working with children, when they were critically ill and faced the possibility of dying.

That was hard for him.

It made him think of the child he'd never got to hold.

The child that was lost to him.

Ryan stopped and took a deep breath. He couldn't think about that. Right now, he had to focus on that little girl, who was scared.

He stopped at the main nurses' station.

"Do you happen to have Dr. Emily West's phone number? I need to send her a message."

"She's still here, Dr. Gary."

"What?"

"She's in on-call room four."

"Thanks." Ryan cursed under his breath. What was

she still doing at the hospital? She was supposed to go home and get some rest. He was annoyed, but not really surprised. Surgeons liked to push themselves and a pregnant surgeon was no different.

A doctor or a surgeon would tell their patient to take it easy but wouldn't always listen to their own cues to take a break. How many times had he gone without sleep or food because of a patient? He couldn't let Emily put that kind of strain on her body.

He knocked gently on the on-call room's door, but there was no answer. He turned the knob slowly and peeked inside the darkened room. In the light from the open door he could see her curled up on her side, sleeping peacefully.

All the annoyance that he was feeling toward her for not going home to rest melted away as he watched her sleeping peacefully in the dark. He walked over to her and knelt down beside her. She was really beautiful, stubborn, smart. There was so much he liked about her.

It was why he'd been so drawn to her the first time he'd met her.

He reached out and gently touched her round belly. There was a tiny movement under his palm and his heart skipped a beat. He felt a rush of emotion. What made him think that he could be a father? He couldn't be a father. It was better that he just sign the divorce papers and let it go.

He'd been hurt when Morgan had terminated her pregnancy eight years ago. She hadn't wanted to be a mother and she hadn't believed he had what it took to be a father because he had never been around. She'd respected his career and Morgan had wanted a career more than family. Perhaps Morgan was right. He loved his career over everything. He didn't know how to be a father because he hadn't had one to learn from.

Get a hold of yourself.

She moaned in her sleep and he took his hand back.

Ryan stood up and moved away. He didn't want her to wake up and see him hovering over her in the dark.

He knocked on the open door and she stirred, opening her eyes.

"Ryan?"

"Sorry, I didn't mean to wake you. I thought you'd gone home."

Emily sat up and rubbed her eyes. "I was going to, but I was worried about Raquel."

Ryan sighed. "There's a mass in her brain. I won't know until I do a biopsy."

Emily's face fell. "Oh, how awful."

"I'm letting them rest tonight and I'll do the biopsy tomorrow."

Emily glanced at the alarm clock on the table. "It is tomorrow."

"Okay, then later today," Ryan joked.

"After the mother of the conjoined twins arrives. We need to meet with Dr. Samuel, the OB/GYN on the case, in an online session with Dr. Ruchi to talk about when the babies will be delivered and how we'll proceed."

Ryan nodded. "I understand that and in order to do that you need to go home and get some rest."

Her shoulders drooped. "I can sleep here. It's fine."

Ryan shook his head. "You'll be more comfortable in your own bed. Let me take you home and we can discuss Raquel's case on the way."

She opened her mouth like she was going to argue with him, but then let out another exhausted sigh. "Okay."

"Okay?" he asked in shock. "You're actually agreeing with me?"

She gave him a look like he was crazy. "Don't make me change my mind."

He chuckled. "Come on. Let's get you home."

Ryan grabbed her coat and his. They left the hospital together. It was drizzling and damp, completely different from San Diego, where he'd returned to after his spell in the Middle East, and also completely different from Wyoming.

Wyoming was cold and dry. At least where he'd lived, where there were vast open spaces and buttes from the badlands. It was like Mother Nature had scoured everything good away to the harsh, cold rock beneath. Growing up, he'd always felt lonely there.

Because you were lonely.

He shook that thought away. Right now, he didn't want to think about his mother. But, then again, he never wanted to think about his mother.

"My car is over here."

"Do you want me to drive?" he asked.

Emily cocked an eyebrow. "Do you know where I live?"

"Good point." He opened her door and then went around to the passenger side.

"I don't live far and I really need to be back at the hospital for nine."

"I want to be back for rounds at seven," Ryan said. "I'll just take a taxi back to the hospital once I make sure that you're settled in for the night. It's been a long day."

Emily nodded. "That I can agree with."

Emily was right, it wasn't a long drive to her apartment. Ryan followed her inside and made sure she got up to her apartment. It was late at night and there was no doorman at her apartment complex.

She opened the door and flicked on the lights. Her apartment was sparse, like she was barely home, but it had beautiful floor-to-ceiling windows that faced the Space Needle and the sound.

"This is a great place."

"Yeah, it's okay. It's just an apartment." She took off her coat. "You wanted to talk about Raquel?"

Ryan nodded as he shut the door and locked it. "I did."

Emily sat down on the couch and he took a seat in the chair next to the couch. "The MRI showed a tumor pressing on the occipital lobe."

"So it could be a meningioma?" Emily asked. "That is the most common in a primary brain tumor."

"I'm hoping that's what it is. Something that I could easily handle." Ryan scrubbed a hand over his face. "I won't know until I get in there and do a biopsy. I hate having to biopsies on kids."

Emily's expression softened. "It's not one of my favorite parts of the job."

"No." He leaned back in the chair. "I would like you in there while I do the biopsy."

"Do you really need me in there?" she asked. "A resident could easily assist you."

He gazed at her. "I don't trust anyone else. I trust you."

The admission caught her off guard.

He trusted her?

How could he trust her? He didn't even know her. Except for that one night and today together, they knew nothing about each other, and you couldn't form a bond of trust that fast.

"Ryan, you don't even know me."

"I know how you work in an operating room," he said quickly. "That's why."

She let out an inward sigh of relief. So that's what he'd meant and she could respect that. "You'll never learn how the other surgeons work in your operating room if you don't work with them. We have some of the best and most dedicated residents and fellows in our teaching program. If you trust me, you'll believe me that they're worth their salt and it would mean so much to our teaching program if they could assist Dr. Ryan Gary in a procedure."

A smile tugged at the corners of his lips.

She knew how to stroke an ego. Another social cue she'd learned well. It had gotten her far in her career.

"You're just buttering me up. I know your modus operandi."

Emily chuckled softly. "Well, it's the truth. Besides, we're going to need a large team to do this conjoined twin separation and there are going to be a lot of moving pieces in this surgery. It's best you start working with my staff, with my residents."

"You have a point."

"I know I do," she replied saucily.

He shook his head. "So, are you ever going to go to bed? It's past one in the morning."

"You're right. You'd better call your cab."

"If you don't mind, I might crash for a couple of minutes on your couch."

Emily glanced at the couch. "It's not that comfortable. It's pretty old."

"It'll be fine."

"Okay, then sure. Just wake me before you go to catch the first set of rounds. I want to get up and start the day too."

Ryan nodded. "I promise."

"I'll get you a blanket and a pillow."

Ryan peeled off his coat and kicked off his shoes as he settled down on her old couch. "Thanks."

Emily walked down the hall to the linen closet and pulled out an extra blanket and pillow. By the time she got back to the living room Ryan was flat on his back and fast asleep. She couldn't help but smile as she watched him sleep.

If someone had told her a couple of days ago that her one-night stand and father of her baby would be crashing on her couch and she was actually letting him do that, she would've thought that person was crazy.

Maybe I am *crazy.*

She shook her head and then set the pillow down on the chair. She unfolded the blanket and gently laid it over him. It had been a long, emotional day.

The day hadn't been boring. It had been a whirlwind. Just like that night in Vegas that they'd spent together.

She sighed and then left the living room. She needed to get some sleep if she was going to wake up by the first rounds of the morning, and tomorrow was going to be a long, long day.

Ryan heard crying.

It startled him and he woke up.

Where am I?

He sat up and could see the sky just starting to grow light. It was reflected in the windows of the city and the Space Needle still had its lights flashing. Then he remembered that he was in Seattle and that he was in Emily's apartment.

He heard the cry again and he got up, looking for Emily.

Oh, God. Please don't be the baby.

His first thought was that she'd pushed it too far and that he'd have to rush her to the hospital, but when he found her she was curled up on one side and sleeping. She was dreaming.

Ryan let out a sigh of relief and scrubbed a hand over his face. He glanced at her alarm clock and saw that it was five-thirty in the morning. The first set of rounds at SMFPC started promptly at seven.

At least she was close to the hospital. He wanted to let her sleep because he was planning to leave, but she'd made him promise to wake her when he was going to leave.

He crept over to the bed and knelt down, gently touching her.

"Emily?"

"Nope," she snarled, and rolled over, continuing to snore loudly into her pillow.

A smile quirked his mouth. "Emily? You wanted to know when I was going to leave."

"Shut up," she mumbled into her pillow.

He laughed. She was feisty in her sleep. He liked that. "Emily?"

"Just get into bed and shut up!" she snapped, sitting up with her eyes wide open, before she lay back down.

Ryan shrugged and climbed into the bed next to her. He'd give her a few more minutes and then he would try and wake her up again. Her bed was really comfortable and as he sank down next to her she snuggled up against him.

She was so warm and his eyelids were getting awfully heavy.

Stay awake. Stay awake.

Ryan tried to keep himself awake by thinking about the biopsy, about the conjoined twin case and about Jason. He thought about the job offer that was waiting for him in San Diego, the one that he was stalling on taking because he really didn't want to settle down anywhere.

Except that wasn't working. All he could think about in this moment was that Emily was beside him and how warm she was.

Stay awake.

He scrubbed a hand over his face and yawned quietly into his fist. His body ached from sleeping on her horrible couch and he was worn out from constantly moving around. Maybe it would be good to settle down and he was annoyed that he was thinking about that.

His body was like lead and it felt like he was sinking into her mattress. He really should get up and leave. He should find a coffee cart and order a triple shot of espresso.

Come on. Stay awake.

Only he couldn't and he prayed that he didn't give Emily a complete fright when she woke up next to him in about an hour.

CHAPTER SIX

EMILY WOKE WHEN her alarm went off. It was six thirty and rounding would start soon. She thought that Ryan would've woken her.

When she rolled over she was startled when she saw that Ryan was lying on top of her duvet and fast asleep.

How had he got in here? And, more importantly, when had he got here?

"Ryan," she said, shaking him. "Wake up, you're going to be late for rounds."

"What?" Ryan sat bolt upright and rubbed his eyes. "Oh, my God, I fell asleep."

"Yeah, I was meaning to ask you how it came to be that you're in my bed," she said incredulously.

"You invited me," he said, stifling a yawn, before he shimmied to the edge of the bed.

"Pardon?" she asked, not really hearing him. "I invited you?"

He nodded. "You did."

"I don't remember that at all. The last thing I remember was that you were passed out on my couch, sound asleep, and I went to bed. Alone."

"Yes, but then I heard you crying."

"I wasn't crying," she said indignantly.

"You were crying in your sleep. I tried to wake you to tell you that I was leaving but you told me to shut up repeatedly. You also said no several times and then you told me to get into bed with you. You sat right up, looked me in the eye and told me to get into bed with you. Who was I to argue?"

There was a smug grin on his face and she groaned.

"I don't remember any of that at all."

She'd had the propensity for night terrors and talking in her sleep when she'd been younger, but as far as she knew she hadn't done it in a while. She only used to do it when she'd been really stressed out.

When she'd been completely overloaded by the rest of the world. When interaction with people and stressful situations had been too much for her Asperger's, the night terrors had always come. Robert had hated the night terrors. He would complain bitterly about them.

Emily buried her head in her arms. "Ugh. I'm so sorry."

"Don't be sorry." His statement caught her off guard. It made her relax. No one had ever said she didn't have to apologize when she was feeling overloaded and overwhelmed. It was nice to feel accepted.

"Besides, your bed is very comfortable and I was exhausted."

Emily chuckled. She knew he got up when the weight on the mattress shifted. She looked up to see him pulling on his coat, which he'd left at the foot of the bed, obviously when he'd come to tell her he was leaving and her unconscious self had told him to get into bed!

"If you give me ten minutes I can be ready and we can head to the hospital together. I'm sorry for making

you late for rounds by demanding you sleep with me."
It was a subtle attempt at a joke.

He smiled at her. "It's okay. Take your time. I'm going
to call a cab and get to the hospital so that I can talk to
Raquel's mother and have a resident assist me in Raquel's
biopsy."

Emily felt a sense of relief and sank back against her
pillows, but still sitting upright. "Thank you for taking
my talk about teaching our residents so seriously."

"So, who would you recommend?"

"Dr. Sharipova, and he should be there already. He's
probably read Raquel's chart and familiarized himself
with it."

Ryan nodded. "He's eager. I do like that."

"Let him lead. Dr. Teal is one of his interns and Dr.
Sharipova has seniority over her."

"I will. I don't want to step on any toes. It's been some
time since I worked in a teaching hospital."

"It's okay. You're forgiven" she teased. "You'd better
go or traffic will make you late."

Ryan nodded. "I'll see you later?"

"Yes. I'll have you paged when the patient from Portland is coming in."

"Okay." Ryan hesitated for a moment, like he wanted
to say something else, but he didn't. He just ducked his
head. "See you."

Emily craned her neck and watched him as he pulled
on his shoes and left her bedroom. Then she heard the
door being unlocked, opened and shut again.

She leaned back against the pillows and closed her
eyes. She was annoyed that she'd asked him to sleep with
her, but it explained why she'd slept so well. It had been

months since she'd slept so deeply. It felt really good to get a really deep sleep, even if it was of a short duration.

You can't let him in.

And she had to keep reminding herself of that. She couldn't let him in. The last time she'd let someone in, she'd been so hurt.

"What do you mean, you got the lead attending position in Seattle?" Robert demanded. "How could someone like you get it?"

His words were like a slap in the face. "What do you mean, someone like me?"

"On the spectrum."

She ignored his hateful words. He was angry. He often used it against her when he was stressed and angry. He took advantage of the fact that she struggled to read social cues. Besides, when she'd found out he was cheating on her too she knew she had to get away from this toxic environment, which was why she'd applied for the job.

"I applied for it and Dr. Ruchi recommended me..."

"Oh, of course Dr. Ruchi would recommend you. She hates me. You remember how she treated me when we were interns. She threw her recommendation away on someone who barely passed the surgical boards!"

His hateful words had crushed her heart and her spirit. She had been so depressed and it had been Dr. Ruchi who had talked sense into her and brought her out of her slump. Ana had put her on the right path to focus on her career.

It was the kick in the butt that she had needed.

She'd managed to keep her head together for five years, until she'd met Ryan.

And he'd been in Seattle for less than twenty-four

hours and he'd already been in her bed again. What was it about him? Why did she have such a weakness for him?

The baby moved and Emily couldn't help but smile and touch her belly.

"It's you, isn't it? You're the one messing with the rational side of my brain." It was a joke.

The baby poked at her and she laughed softly to herself. She knew why she had a weakness for Ryan. He was confident in everything he did. He was comfortable in his own skin. He was strong and sure of himself. He was smart and passionate about his career and he seemed to care. Robert had never cared and she was angry at herself for not seeing it earlier.

She had to get up, have a shower and get something to eat. Today was going to be a long day and she wanted to be fighting ready when the mother of the conjoined twins arrived. She wanted to be able to assure her patient that they had a plan in place to take care of her babies when they were born.

The problem was, she didn't have a plan in place and she needed to talk to Dr. Samuel and put a plan in place, because the first step was making sure that both of the babies survived their birth and were stable and stronger before she even attempted to separate them.

She didn't have time to think about Ryan or the fact that he'd been in her bed.

Or the fact that she was glad he'd been there.

Ryan drank down his second triple espresso. His hand was shaking and he was trying to regain control over his emotions. He hated it when kids cried.

He hated it when anyone cried.

It reminded him of his father and how his father would

always lay into him when he cried, which was why he tried not to do it.

His mother had also used to tell him that it had been his crying as a child that had caused his father to leave. It hadn't just been him crying. His dad hadn't wanted to ranch, and his mother had. It was just like him not wanting to stay on the land either.

"Fine," his mother had snapped when she'd learned about his acceptance at Harvard. "Leave, but don't come back!"

It had hurt him, but he'd listened to her.

So he hated seeing a kid so hurt or scared that they cried. He was worried that something bad would happen to them, though he knew that wasn't the case.

Parents usually weren't like that, but it was just a deep-rooted reaction he was still trying hard to get rid of.

Raquel had every right to be terrified.

He was going to have to do a stereotactic brain biopsy, which meant taking tissue out of her head, which meant an operation. Any child would be terrified. At least he'd been able to assure her that she'd be asleep.

That had eased her fears.

Still, her crying and his lack of sleep had set his nerves on edge and he needed to find a quiet place to calm down and think. He also needed another espresso.

He finished his coffee and threw the paper cup in the garbage.

"Dr. Gary, I have the operating room ready."

Ryan looked over to see Dr. Sharipova standing beside him.

"Good, and has the patient been prepped?" Ryan asked.

"My intern, Dr. Teal, is doing that now."

"Good. I'll go up and see them right now." Ryan headed toward the pediatric inpatient ward. It was the ward at SMFPC that was used to house the kids who were waiting. Waiting for test results, waiting for general surgery, waiting for answers.

It would take some time to test Raquel's biopsy and he hoped that he didn't have to move Raquel to the cancer ward. He never liked having to diagnose cancer.

Raquel looked terrified and Dr. Teal had finished prepping her for surgery. Ryan had promised that Raquel would get an IV only after she went to sleep, and it was standard procedure for SMFPC, as was parental presence at induction.

"How are we doing?" Ryan asked, mustering the best smile that he could for the frightened little girl.

Raquel just shook her head and wouldn't look at him.

"Dr. Teal, would you give us a moment?" Ryan asked.

"Of course, Dr. Gary." Dr. Teal left the room.

"What's up?" Ryan asked. "You know that you can ask me anything."

"I don't want you to shave my head," Raquel whispered.

"That's it?" Ryan asked.

Raquel nodded. "Dr. Teal said you'd have to shave my head."

"Only a small part, just so I can do the biopsy. Very small."

Raquel stared at him, her dark brown eyes questioning, and he could tell that she didn't quite believe him.

"The needle is small, very small, and I just need to make a tiny little incision and a tiny little hole in your skull to sneak out my sample. I promise you, you won't have a bald patch, but I do need to put in some stitches."

"See, baby? It's okay," Raquel's mother said gently.

"Okay, just don't shave my entire head," Raquel said.

Ryan smiled gently at her. "I promise. If I have to shave your entire head, you can shave my head."

Raquel's eyes lit up. "Really?"

Ryan nodded. "Yep."

"Deal!" Raquel agreed eagerly.

"That's a good deal." Ryan turned to Raquel's mother. "You're willing to participate in the parental presence at induction?"

"I am. Raquel wants me there."

He nodded. "Good. It does help calm them. I am a supporter of parental presence at induction. I'm going to have a child life support worker come up here very soon and prepare you both for surgery. A child life support worker can help calm kids before and after, and she'll help you too. As you know, I'm doing a stereotactic biopsy.

"I place small markers on your head to help guide the CT scan and find that lesion on your brain that I saw in the MRI. The one that has been causing your seizures and your other symptoms. You'll be asleep during that and once I find that spot I shave a minuscule patch of hair, make my incision and then make a small hole in the skull to take my samples. After I have my samples, we close you all back up and we wait for results."

Raquel's mother squeezed her daughter's hand. "Okay."

Her voice shook and Ryan couldn't really blame her. It was not a fun procedure and he'd already explained the possible complications to Raquel's mother, away from Raquel. His young patient didn't need to hear about the chance of cancer or intracranial pressure and hemorrhages.

"I'll leave you both to it and I'll see you soon in the operating room."

"Have your clippers ready," Raquel teased.

Ryan winked at the little girl and then left the room. Dr. Teal was waiting nearby.

"Dr. Teal, send a child life support person up to help Raquel's mother prepare for the parental presence at induction. Her mom needs to be dressed in scrubs before she can enter the OR."

"Right away, Dr. Gary. And I received a page from Dr. West. It seems like the patient from Portland is arriving in ambulance bay three. Dr. Samuel and Dr. West were hoping that you could join them there before your biopsy."

"Dr. Samuel?" Ryan asked, feeling a slight pang of jealousy and worried that Emily had replaced him with someone else.

"He's the OB/GYN on the case."

"Oh, good. Yes, I'll head down there right now. Thank you, Dr. Teal."

Ryan turned and started walking toward the ambulance bay. It would serve him right for Emily to replace him. He could understand her need to plan the separation surgery and he had been pushing her off because he wanted to talk about their night in Vegas.

"You're a selfish child!" his mother screamed at him. *"No wonder your father left us."*

Ryan shook that thought from his head. He was angry that all these memories were deciding to come back out of the blue. They were very unwelcome.

Why was he thinking about this stuff now?

What was it about seeing Emily and being in Seattle that was doing this to him? He hadn't thought of his parents in years.

That's because you never stand still long enough to let them in.

And that was it. He never sat still. He was always in demand. Always being offered cases and consults all over North America and sometimes overseas.

He didn't have a place to call home.

He didn't have any roots.

It wasn't for lack of offers. He always had tons of offers, but he didn't want to settle down anywhere. The only twice he'd been really settled in his life had been in his childhood and in his relationship with Morgan. Both had ended badly.

His mother had disowned him. Morgan had left him and terminated her pregnancy because she'd wanted to focus on career.

Ryan closed his eyes and clenched his fist, taking a deep, calming breath. Maybe Morgan had been right. How could he be a good father when he was always on the move? When he had no real father figure to model himself on?

When he walked into the ambulance bay he saw Emily standing there, waiting for the patient and scrolling through a tablet. Probably going through patient information. Her short blonde hair was pinned back and she looked well rested.

Good.

And then he focused on her round belly and his heart clenched.

How can I be a good father?

And he couldn't help but think that maybe his child would be better off without him.

Emily would be better off without him.

And he would have to keep reminding himself that this was just a professional relationship, because once the twins were separated he'd move on somewhere else.

That's what he always did.

And he didn't see a change to that.

Emily looked up because she felt like someone was staring at her. She saw Ryan lingering just outside the ambulance bay. He looked exhausted and she felt slightly bad, because she was pretty sure that she was the cause of it.

Her sister always said that when they shared a room that she hardly ever got sleep because Emily talked loudly in her sleep about random things.

Well, Ryan would be able to get sleep tonight because that was the first and last time he would be at her apartment and sleeping in her bed. There had to be boundaries. If they were going to keep this relationship strictly professional they had to stop having dinner together, ending up in bed together!

There had to be rules to follow but, then, there was a part of her that secretly loved the fact she had slept so well.

That someone cared about her again.

Don't get sucked into that trap again.

Emily looked away as Ryan started walking toward her. She had to collect her thoughts, she couldn't think about how nice it had been to wake up snuggled up against him. How she'd enjoyed their brief dinner last night in the bistro or how she appreciated that he'd bought her a sandwich and made sure that she was taking care of herself.

"Dr. West, I was told that our patient is arriving from Portland," he said, and she was relieved that he used her professional name in front of Dr. Samuel. Dr. Samuel was her OB/GYN as well and she hadn't told him that Ryan was the father of her child.

Of course, that might be common knowledge after he'd announced in front of Dr. Teal that they were married.

"Yes, the ambulance is about fifteen minutes out," Emily said, clearing her throat and suddenly feeling very awkward. "Dr. Samuel, this is Dr. Ryan Gary, the neurosurgeon who will be doing the separation surgery with me."

Dr. Samuel's eyes lit up. "I'm very familiar with Dr. Gary's work. It's a pleasure."

Ryan shook Dr. Samuel's hand. "Very pleased to meet you."

"Derek," Samuel responded. "And I understand that you're the father of Emily's baby and her husband. I didn't know that Emily was married, but that's not surprising. She tends to keep things quiet. Belated congratulations on your marriage and the baby."

Ryan cocked an eyebrow and looked at her. Emily felt heat bloom in her cheeks.

Yep. word had gotten around the hospital.

"Derek..." Emily trailed off because she didn't know what to say.

"Thank you," Ryan responded gracefully. "We're excited."

Derek smiled and nodded. "Well, we have an ultrasound in a few days. I hope you'll still be around by then to come. Emotional support for the expectant mother is imperative in the birthing process."

"I couldn't agree more," Ryan said. And he felt a twinge of guilt. Would he even be here in three months when she gave birth? He wasn't sure.

Emily groaned and walked away from them. This was not keeping things professional or discreet at all.

And then she heard the distant wail of the ambulance. The transport was here and Emily had to put aside all her personal feelings about Ryan, about the baby, about everything at this moment.

This case was her top priority and she had to be make sure their patient was comfortable and not in distress. They had to keep the babies in utero as long as possible, so they would be born stronger and would have a better shot at surviving their surgery.

That was all that mattered at this moment.

CHAPTER SEVEN

EMILY WAITED OUTSIDE while Dr. Samuel assessed Janet, the mother of the conjoined twins, and talked to the patient about how they were going to proceed with the C-section when the time came. Emily had introduced herself, but she didn't want to overwhelm Janet and talk about the separation surgery just yet.

It was clear, on her arrival, that Janet was stressed out and scared. Emily understood those overwhelming feelings all too well.

Not that Emily could blame her in the slightest. She reached down and touched her belly. Her baby was quiet right now and that was okay.

"How is she doing?" Ryan asked.

"I think she's calming down. She was stressed and her blood pressure was up. Dr. Samuel is worried Janet is developing pre-eclampsia."

Ryan winced. "That's not good. Although I don't blame her for feeling stressed. She's been moved to another city, another state and her other child is back in Oregon. Their life is on hold and she's not even sure that in the end it will pay off, that her babies will survive."

"That's kind of dour," Emily said.

Ryan shrugged. "It's the truth, though."

She sighed.

He was right. It was the truth and it sucked.

"Aren't you supposed to be doing a biopsy?" she asked.

"I'm on my way there right now. Raquel is on her way to the operating room. Do you want to come? You don't have to assist, but maybe see Raquel's test through to the end? You were the one who was there when she was having her seizure. You kept your cool and helped me get her on her side, propping her head up."

Emily was torn. She really wanted to be there for Raquel, but she also wanted to keep her distance from Ryan.

This is just a procedure and Raquel is a patient. There's no harm.

"Okay. I would like observe. I'll sit in the gallery."

"I'm not doing this surgery in the OR with a gallery, so you'll have to scrub in." There was a devious twinkle in his eyes, as if he'd planned it.

"Of course not. Fine. I'll scrub in."

"Good. Let's go."

Emily nodded and followed Ryan to the OR floor. They changed into the surgical scrubs and Emily tied on her scrub cap, tucking her short hair up underneath. They made their way to the smaller operating room at the end of the OR floor. Raquel was waiting in the hallway. Her mother was standing next to her, wearing her scrubs. She was holding her daughter's hand and the child life support person was with them.

Emily smiled and went over to see them while Ryan started his scrub in.

"How are you doing, Raquel?" Emily asked.

"Good," Raquel responded.

"Do you remember who I am?" Emily asked.

"No, I'm sorry, but Mom told me you were there with Dr. Ryan."

Emily nodded. "I was and I'm going to be in the operating room with him. I'm going to make sure he does his job well."

"Oh, good," Raquel said. "You have to make sure he doesn't completely shave my head."

Emily cocked an eyebrow while Raquel's mother laughed.

"I think I'm missing something," Emily said.

"Dr. Ryan and I made a bet. If he has to shave off all my hair I get to shave his head."

Emily chuckled. "Well, that's a good bet to make. I'll watch him, I promise."

Raquel nodded.

"I'll see you in there." Emily winked and headed into the scrub room. Ryan was just finishing up his scrubbing. Her heart skipped a beat. Of course he would make a bet like that with a child. It was endearing and it was one of the reasons she'd fallen for him six months ago.

"What's so funny?" he asked.

"I heard about your bet," she teased, and she turned on the tap.

He groaned and laughed. "Well, she was pretty worried about it."

"It's sweet."

Ryan rolled his eyes. "Well, thankfully she won't get a chance to shave my head. I'm really hoping for a benign growth."

"Me too."

Ryan headed into the OR as Raquel was rolled in. Emily finished her scrubbing in and stood to the side as Raquel was helped off her gurney onto the operating table. Dr. Sharipova stepped up and announced to the room who Raquel was and what they were doing. Raquel's eyes were wide and she was staring at Dr. Sharipova like he was a monster under the bed.

Emily stepped forward and stood next to Raquel's mother.

"Don't worry, that's just so we make sure we're shaving the right person's head."

Raquel laughed and Emily winked at her from behind her mask.

Dr. Ahmed stepped up. "We're ready to start induction."

Emily nodded and stepped back as a mask was placed over Emily's face and she began to breathe in the anesthetic, counting. Raquel's mother held her daughter's hand and spoke to her. Raquel's grip began to loosen and then suddenly she began to seize.

Raquel's mother cried out.

"Do something!" she cried.

Emily held her. "It's not a seizure like before See, her monitors aren't going off. This is called the excitement phase of anesthetic. It's different for every kid and she's okay. See, she's relaxed."

"She's under now," Dr. Ahmed said. "We're going to set up her IV now."

The child life support person, Patricia, put her arm around Raquel's shaking mother and led her out of the operating room, reassuring her that Raquel would be okay. And she would be.

Emily's emotions were running a bit high.

The excitement phase of general anesthetic could be scary if you were not used to it and even when the child was out, their eyes stayed open with a blank stare that could be unnerving, but by the time Emily turned around the anesthesiologist had inserted the IV, Raquel had been intubated, and her eyelids taped shut. She was put into position and Ryan directed Dr. Sharipova to place the fiducials for the CT scanner on Raquel's head.

It was a frameless technique now, compared to the old way. The small sensors would work like a GPS so that Ryan could find the exact place to cut and extract his sample.

Once the fiducials were placed, Emily took a step back so that she could see the CT scan and watch from a distance.

It didn't take Ryan long before he found his spot and she got to see the lesion on the screen. Her heart sank and she felt tears sting her eyes as she thought of that little girl on the table having to go through this.

It was one of the hardest parts of her job. She didn't want to think about the alternative. That was too scary to even comprehend.

Dr. Sharipova picked up the razor.

"Better let me do that," Ryan said. "I have a bet to win."

Emily chuckled and Ryan looked over his shoulder at her, his blue eyes crinkling at the corners behind the mask.

"What do you get if you win?" Emily asked.

"I get to keep the hair on my head. I thought that was obvious."

"Good deal," she said.

Ryan nodded and shaved off a tiny bit of Raquel's hair. It was underneath and the hair on top would hide it, and unless she braided her hair or pulled it back tightly, you wouldn't even know it was there.

"I think I won this bet."

Emily crept closer and looked. "I believe so, Dr. Gary."

Ryan set the razor down. "Ten blade, please."

The scrub nurse handed him the scalpel and Emily took a step back to watch the CT screen. Ryan had enough people hovering around him as he worked in the small space to retrieve a small sample of tissue.

The brain was so delicate. It was why she hadn't wanted to pursue that path. As a surgical intern in her first year she'd worked on every case. Interns weren't allowed to specialize and the brain and she'd found the nerves were very intimidating.

She'd even thought Pediatrics was intimidating, until Dr. Ruchi had seen the promise in her and sent her in the right direction when she'd been a resident. Emily had never thought she had the knack when it came to kids, because she'd never really planned on having kids, but for some reason pediatrics was her forte.

Helping kids, sick kids, was her passion. Perhaps because she'd had different needs as a child. She wanted to help, and advocate for those who couldn't.

"Dropping in the biopsy needle now," Ryan said.

Emily stared up at the screen and watched on the CT as a thin stereotactic needle was placed into Raquel's brain. It was mesmerizing to watch Ryan gently guide the probe.

"There we go," Ryan whispered. "Perfect."

It didn't take long for him to obtain his samples. He gently retracted the biopsy needle and handed it to Dr. Sharipova.

"Make sure this gets to Pathology. I want a result as soon as possible."

"Of course, Dr. Gary." Dr. Sharipova bagged the sample and then left the operating room. Ryan may want the results fast, but it would take three to four days before they got them.

"All right, let's close her up."

Emily stepped up in Dr. Sharipova's place.

"I thought you might want a hand since you lost your resident," she said.

"Thank you."

"Excellent work." Heat bloomed in her cheeks and she was glad that her blush was hidden by her surgical mask.

"Thank you," Ryan said. "Now, this is the hardest part. Waiting."

Emily nodded.

She understood that.

A lot of this job was hurry up and wait. She was used to the hustle and bustle of hurry up, it's what happened on the other end that was important. Whether or not Raquel had cancer or if the tumor was benign.

Emily was hoping for the latter.

Ryan sat next to Raquel's bedside in the PACU. She would have a really bad headache when she woke up and it would be hard to do a lot of simple tasks while her brain healed. And there was also the risk of intracranial pressure building or an infection.

All he could do was wait and see.

So he charted.

It was somewhat quiet in the PACU. There were other kids coming out of surgery and some were a bit loopy and some were screaming and shouting. You never knew what would happen when people came out of anesthetic.

Parents were allowed in the PACU as SMFPC believed that parental presence was an important part of the healing process. He really liked that about this place. He couldn't even begin to fathom what the parents were going through in the waiting room.

You can't fathom it because you're not a father.

A lump formed in his throat and he shook that thought away. It hurt too much to think of that moment.

Morgan hadn't wanted to have a child.

And that had been the end of that.

Raquel began to stir and whimper.

Ryan turned to the nurse in charge of Raquel.

"You can let her mother come in now."

"Right away, Dr. Gary." The nurse left to tell a volunteer to go and get Raquel's mother.

Ryan closed the chart and set it on the bedside table next to the nurse's computer. He gently touched Raquel.

"Hurts," Raquel mumbled.

"I know. It will," he said gently.

Raquel then reached up and touched. "I have hair?"

"I told you you would."

Raquel smiled. "Guess you win."

"I think we both did. You did really well, Raquel. You're very brave."

Raquel nodded, but wouldn't open her eyes. She just held his hand and it wasn't long before Raquel's mother came into the PACU. He could see the relief on her face as she came to the bedside.

"Baby, I'm here," she whispered.

Raquel nodded.

"She's still a bit groggy from the anesthetic. She did

beautifully," Ryan said. "I want to keep her here for a couple of days. I just want to make sure that she doesn't have any side effects from the biopsy. We should have an answer from Pathology before too long."

"Thank you, Dr. Gary," Raquel's mother said.

"My pleasure. If you have any other questions, please have someone page me."

"I will." Raquel's mother turned back to her daughter and Ryan let go of Raquel's hand. The nurse had been informed about how he wanted her to proceed in the PACU before Raquel was transferred back to her room in the ward.

Ryan's job was done here. For now.

And he hoped that this was all he had to do. If the growth was benign, they could control it through medication.

If it was cancer he would have to do surgery and talk to Oncology about radiation and chemotherapy. Stuff he didn't want to put any child through, but he would cross that bridge if and when the time came.

Right now, he wasn't going to dwell on it.

There was no point in dwelling on the negative.

He left the PACU and headed straight for the cafeteria. He needed to get another cup of coffee and he needed some lunch.

On his way there he saw Emily sitting behind the charge desk, staring at a computer screen. She looked tired again.

"Hey," he said as he walked over to her.

She looked up and her spine stiffened. "Hi."

"Am I interrupting you?"

"No, just going through some research. Trying to

put together a team and book some time in the simulation lab."

"Raquel is in PACU and doing well. Her mother is with her."

A small smile tugged at the corners of her lips. "I'm so glad."

"I'm going to get something to eat in the cafeteria. Do you want to join me?"

Emily hesitated, remembering the vow she'd made to herself to put some distance between them, but only for a moment. Well, she had to eat, didn't she? And maybe they could talk in more detail about the separation operation. "Sure."

She logged off the computer and grabbed her white lab coat, which was on the chair behind her.

"What're you doing for the rest of the day?" he asked.

"Besides prepping for this surgery? I have some rounds later, but the chief of surgery wants my sole focus to be on the conjoined twins and getting ready for that. How about you?"

"Rounds. I need to check on Jason. He's doing well..." He trailed off. Jason was awake, but there was no sign of movement in his legs.

That could also be from the pain medication. Surgery on the spine and spinal cord was intense. Even adults who had spinal surgery were kept pretty medicated for the first few days afterwards.

Ryan was really hoping that it was the pain medication that was causing the delay in motor response. He was just worried because kids always bounced back faster than adults.

"I'm sure it'll be fine. He responded well to your treatment."

It was nice that Emily was trying to be supportive, but he knew how she felt about the therapeutic hypothermia. She'd made that quite clear when he'd first arrived at SMFPC. He was actually surprised she wasn't berating him.

"I'm sure it will," he said, clearing his throat, and decided to change the subject. He didn't want to talk about cases. He needed to lighten the mood. "So, anything I should see in Seattle before I leave?"

A strange expression crossed her face when he mentioned leaving, but it was fleeting.

"Well, there's the Space Needle and you should take a ferry ride. There's also the market and walking down by the sound is always nice. There are houseboats and other interesting things to look at. I really enjoy walking down there."

"How about Mount Rainier? Should I take a day trip to see that?"

Emily shrugged. "I suppose. I've never gone myself. It was something I always wanted to do, I've just never had the time for it."

"Well, maybe we should take a day trip out there? There are enough pediatric surgeons on hand and we should go while everything is quiet."

"Don't say quiet," Emily teased. "It's never quiet and I can't leave. What if Janet, the conjoined twins' mother, goes into early labor? I have to be here to make sure those babies are stable."

"If the babies are born now they won't survive. Maybe if they were single they would have a shot, but conjoined? They need more time. You know that. She's just at twenty-five weeks, not in the third trimester yet. It's why she's on bed rest and Dr. Samuel is monitoring her."

Emily sighed. "Well, I do have the next couple of days off. I was going to do research."

"Do you ever take time for yourself or do you work constantly?" Ryan teased.

"The last time I did something crazy and fun and took time for myself I ended up in a wedding chapel in Vegas."

Ryan laughed. "Right."

"I like work," Emily said quietly as they got into line in the cafeteria.

"I know you do, but you need a day off. Besides, it's not like you can repeat your mistake. We're already married and you're already pregnant."

Emily rolled her eyes, but then laughed. "Yeah, I suppose so."

"So why don't we take a trip out to Mount Rainier National Park and have a picnic? I heard tomorrow is supposed to be decent."

Emily sighed. "You're not going to let this go, are you?"

"You need a break and I need to see some sights before I leave."

"Fine." Emily grabbed a sandwich. "You have to bring the picnic, though, since I have to drive."

"Deal."

They paid for their lunch and made their way to an empty table. The cafeteria was busier than the first time they'd eaten here together, but he was glad of the hustle and bustle.

He was used to hustle and bustle.

It was the quiet and the calm that let in all those bad memories. Thoughts about his lost child, his father and mother all haunted him in the solitude of quiet.

He liked the commotion. He could think in the commotion.

The only thing that was impeding his thoughts right now was being near Emily. He hadn't realized how much she affected him. She got under his skin.

And that scared him, because he didn't want to disappoint her, like he had been disappointed so many times before.

Emily noticed Ryan had gone quiet.

"You okay? You've been staring at your sandwich for a good five minutes."

He shook his head. "Still exhausted from my lack of sleep. I'm not used to being ordered around by an unconscious person."

He was teasing her, she could tell by the way he was smirking and that glint in his blue eyes.

"Ha. Ha."

"You're mean when you're asleep."

"You listened to me," she countered. "I was asleep, you didn't have to listen to me."

"When a woman tells me to get into bed, I listen," he said seductively, which made her heart beat just a bit faster and she could feel the blush that she seemed to be unable to control around him creep up her neck.

Damn him for being so cocky.

She punched him in the arm. "Not cool."

He was laughing at her. "Ow, that hurt."

"Good." She shook her head.

This was not keeping her relationship with him on a professional level and she only hoped that no one around them had heard that comment from him about her ordering him to get into her bed when she was sleeping.

"It was a night terror. That's the only reason I asked you into my bed," she said in a hushed tone.

"It didn't seem like a night terror, but I can see what you mean. You were kind of terrifying, ordering me about and telling me to shut up."

Emily chuckled. "It could've been worse. I could've actually have been screaming. Night terrors are not fun. We have some pediatric patients with them and often have to move them to their own room instead of being in a ward or sharing with someone else."

"I have to say you were my first time dealing with someone who was even close to having night terrors. I don't think I want to deal with a child screaming in their sleep. It's bad enough when they are awake."

"At least you can console them when they're awake. When they're in the throes of a night terror you can't." Emily looked down at her bump and hoped that she wouldn't pass that on to her child. Her child was at risk for inheriting her autism and anxiety. The possibility scared her.

It was going to be hard enough doing this on her own, she didn't need night terrors or sleep-walking added to the mix.

You don't have to do it alone.

She glanced at Ryan. He'd said that he wanted to be involved and so far had refused to sign the divorce papers, but then he said things like he was moving on. He talked like he didn't really want to stay or be a part of their child's life.

How could she rely on him?

She couldn't.

She'd seen what true marriage was with her parents.

They were friends and lovers. They helped each other out and supported each other.

They shared the load.

If she ever thought about getting married, that was the type of marriage she wanted to have. She wanted her husband to be her partner in every sense of the word. Robert hadn't been that person and it appeared that Ryan wasn't either. Surgeons were self-possessed and absorbed.

They were confident, overbearing and sure of themselves.

They had to be.

She was. Lives were in their hands.

Ryan may care about her and care about their child, but he really didn't talk much about their baby. He didn't ask to feel their child move and he talked about moving on. He was a jet-setting world-renowned neurosurgeon and she really doubted that he would ever settle down.

She would let him be involved as much as he wanted, but he was not someone she could rely on for the day-to-day parenting. That would fall to her alone because she had no plans to leave Seattle and really had no desire to live his jet-setting lifestyle.

She was alone in this.

She'd known that the moment the stick had turned blue, but suddenly she was feeling quite unsure about the whole thing.

She had what it took to be a surgeon, but did she really have what it took to be a single parent?

That uncertainty frightened her.

CHAPTER EIGHT

JUST CALL HIM and cancel.

She looked outside and it was a beautiful sunny day in Seattle.

Drat.

Emily had been hoping for miserable weather so she could get out of this day trip to Mount Rainier National Park with Ryan. After their lunch yesterday, she'd gone back to doing her research and then her rounds. She'd managed to avoid him for the rest of the day, because the more she got thinking about him leaving, the more it upset her, and she didn't like that at all. She had been hoping that he'd forget about his brilliant idea to take a day trip, until he'd texted her that he would come and pick her up at nine in the morning.

She'd thought she was supposed to be the one driving, but apparently Ryan had got himself a rental car and was insisting on driving the three hours to the park. What they were going to do there, she had no idea.

There were a couple of short hikes she could manage, but other than that she really didn't know. When she'd lived in Utah, she'd often gone for long hikes. Her favorite place to go had been down to St. George and do the Canaveral Falls hike.

It had been a long time since she'd done anything outdoors like that.

Maybe this will be good? the hopeful side of her thought, whereas the other side of her brain, the doubt weasel portion, told her that this was a huge mistake.

She went to pick up her phone to text him that she wasn't going when the buzzer at the door sounded. It wasn't even nine.

He was early. She wasn't completely prepared mentally yet. It was a struggle sometimes when the set schedule wasn't followed.

Early was better than late.

Emily set down her phone. "Hello?"

"It's me. Ryan. Are you ready?"

"Not quite. You're early. It's not even eight thirty yet."

"Sorry, I didn't realize how fast I would get here. I overcompensated for traffic, which is surprisingly not bad."

Made sense why he was early.

"Come on up." She buzzed him in, while cursing under her breath.

Maybe it won't be so bad?

She'd been in Seattle for five years and she hadn't really seen much of it. She didn't have many friends here. The entire time she'd lived in this city she'd been focused completely on work, so much so that when she'd told the on call pediatric attending that she was going out of town, he'd looked surprised.

That's the way you wanted it. Remember?

She didn't want to form attachments.

It was better to keep everyone at a distance, even if it meant that she was lonely from time to time. Besides, she was used to being alone. Other than her family, she hadn't had many friends growing up.

There was a knock at the door and she opened it.

Ryan looked good in his jeans and flannel shirt. There was a bit of scruff on his face and it suited him. The sight of him all rough and rugged made her feel a bit weak in the knees, but he still looked a bit like a lumberjack.

"Overcompensating?" she teased.

He looked down at his shirt. "What?"

"I didn't know that you owned a flannel buffalo plaid shirt."

"I didn't, but last night I went to an outfitting store and got some stuff. I am from Wyoming, we do have mountains there."

"You still look very lumberjacky," she teased.

He cocked an eyebrow. "Lumberjacky? Is that even a word?"

"Nope, but that's the vibe you're giving off and usually I'm not the best at reading vibes."

Heat bloomed in her cheeks as she realized what she'd let out. No one but Human Resources at SMFPC, Dr. Ruchi and her family knew about her diagnosis.

Robert knew.

And look how that had turned out.

She sat down on the couch and pulled on her hiking shoes. "We're not going on some crazy half-day hike, are we?" She was trying to change the subject so he didn't ask too many questions about her statement.

"No, but there's a short one called Trail of the Shadows that loops through the Longmire Meadow that I thought would be nice. The man at the outfitting store gave me a map of the national park and marked all the geohazards we have to be aware of."

"Geohazards? What geohazards?" Emily asked, suddenly concerned.

"Mount Rainier is a volcano. An active volcano."

"What?"

"Please tell me you knew this."

She rubbed her temples. "I did. I mentally blocked it out."

Great.

Volcanoes kind of freaked her out and deep down she knew there were many volcanoes on the western seaboard because they were in the Cascades region, which was part of the Pacific "ring of fire", but she'd blocked it from her mind that Seattle sat in the shadow of Mount Rainier. It kept her anxiety over volcanoes at bay.

Salt Lake City had mountains, but they were not volcanic.

"Maybe this is a bad idea."

No. You need to face your fear.

She hadn't got where she was by giving in to her anxieties. She could do this.

"It'll be fine. They have a lot of safeties in place, we just have to be aware of the signs."

"Are you aware of the signs?" Emily asked, feeling a bit nervous. "I'm not aware of the signs."

She hated not being prepared.

Deep breath. You've got this.

"Yellowstone is a super-volcano that is full of pits of boiling geothermic water. I'm aware of the signs and I know what to do if a bear comes close as well."

"A bear?" Emily bent down and began to untie her shoes.

"What're you doing?" he asked.

"Nope, not going. Bears and volcanoes."

He laughed at her. She hated that he laughed. Robert would laugh at her when she'd become overwhelmed about something he'd thought was foolish.

"Don't laugh at me. It's not funny. I'm freaking out."

His expression softened. "I'm not laughing at you."

"You're not?"

"No. They're legitimate fears. I was laughing because it was cute. It's nice seeing someone so confident have a fear."

The compliment caught her off guard. She was far from confident. Ryan sat down next to her.

"Mount Rainier isn't going to erupt today. Trust me, I checked the USGS website today. The mountain is quiet."

Emily narrowed her eyes. "Too quiet." She was trying now to make light of it all so he didn't suspect anything about her diagnosis.

He laughed. "Come on. Live a little."

"The last time I did that, I ended up with this!" She pointed to her belly.

"As I said before, I can't knock you up again."

Emily frowned, but then couldn't help but smile. "Fine. I'll go, but if I see lava, we're done."

"Deal, though for the record lava is the last thing you'd see. First you'd feel the earthquake."

"Look, do you not want me to go?"

"I want you to go."

"So let's go and no more talking about things erupting." She grabbed her keys and her purse. Ryan held open the door and shut it when they were in the hall. She locked her apartment and they headed to the elevator.

"Today is a nice day, Emily. It'll be a good day. You'll see."

"Yeah, as long as we don't get attacked by bears or get caught up in some kind of geohazard."

"The last time Mount Rainier erupted was in 1894."

Emily pushed the button. "Are you telling me it's due to erupt?"

Ryan cocked an eyebrow. "You know, for a pediatric surgeon you're a bit of a pessimist."

She couldn't help but smile then. The conversation was light and easy and they were moving away from what she didn't want him to know about her.

People thought differently about her when they knew.

The elevator door opened and she walked on. She would've continued the conversation, but there were other people in the elevator and they didn't need to know about her conversation regarding her irrational fear of Mount Rainier erupting and wreaking havoc on her life.

For the life of her, she didn't know why she didn't equate the volcano with the mountain when one of the emergency simulations they trained for was just that. People in the path of the lahars and the pyroclastic cloud, if Mount Rainier ever decided to blow her top, would be evacuated to Seattle.

They had a lot of contingency plans in place.

Mudslides, massive accidents, wildfires, earthquakes, volcanic eruptions and super-storms. All the exciting natural disasters one could think of when you lived in such a hotbed of activity.

At least they didn't have tornadoes.

Never say never.

She shuddered. She had to stop thinking about things like that or she'd get overwhelmed.

The elevator dinged and they got off at the lobby.

Ryan had parked just in front of her building. He had rented an SUV.

"You really went all out for this trip, didn't you?" she said, impressed.

"I like driving SUVs and pickups. I guess you can take the man out of Wyoming but not Wyoming out of the man."

"Fair enough." A lot of people in Utah opted for the SUV or the pickup truck. Especially in northern Utah.

It made sense to drive something like this up to Mount Rainier National Park and, to be honest, she felt more at ease with his choice in rental. He held open the door for her and she was slightly mystified.

Robert had certainly never held open the doors for her.

It's a social cue. It's proper.

Ryan climbed into the driver's seat and looked at her. "What?"

"You hold open doors for me."

"So?" he asked, confused.

"No one has ever done that for me before. I think it might be a dying art form."

Ryan grinned. "Well, it was the one good thing my father taught me. The only thing really good about him."

He pulled out into Seattle morning traffic and headed to the interstate, his GPS guiding him, which was good because Emily had no idea how to get to Mount Rainier National Park. As they were driving along she noticed he was gripping the steering wheel really tightly. His knuckles were almost white and they had been like that since he'd mentioned his father.

"Do you want to talk?" she asked.

"About what?"

"You've been kind of tense since we left my place. Since you mentioned your father."

Ryan frowned. "I don't like talking about him much."

"Sorry. Has he passed?" Although she seriously doubted that was the issue when he'd said it was the one good thing his father had taught him and the only good thing about his father.

"My father left when I was seven."

"Sorry to hear that."

He shrugged. "I did fine without him, but at least he taught me good manners, I suppose. My mom always said he was charming, which is a good thing given I travel so much and have to make a good impression wherever I go."

"I suppose because you don't build professional rapport with the surgical staff. You wanted me in the operating room with you instead of the resident because you didn't trust Dr. Sharipova. Now, just think if you were at a hospital permanently. You'd be able to build relationships with your colleagues. You'd know who you worked well with and who you didn't."

He glanced at her briefly. "Perhaps, but it's not really my thing. I'd rather see the world. I tried settling down once and it…" There was hesitation there, like he didn't want to talk about it further. "It just didn't work."

"Why?"

"Wasn't for me," he said quickly, but she could tell by the way his jaw was clenched and how he was still white-knuckling the steering wheel that there was more to it than he was letting it on.

Just let it go. Remember, you wanted to keep things just professional.

And she had to keep reminding herself of that.

Prying into his personal life was not how to keep her distance from him and it was apparent to her that he had no plans of sticking around to see the birth of her child. So not only did she have to protect her heart, she had to protect her unborn baby's heart too.

The three-hour drive to Mount Rainier was mostly un-eventful and Emily dozed off when they were on the interstate. Only when they pulled off the interstate and started winding their way on highway seven did the ride become slightly more scenic and interesting.

"Ohop Bob?" Ryan asked as they drove through a town. "What a strange name."

"They have a pioneer museum!"

"You seem really excited about that. Do you want to stop?"

She shook her head. "No, we should get to the park and then make our way back."

"You really can't stand being away from work, can you?"

"What is that supposed to mean?" she asked.

"It means exactly what I said it means. You just want to turn around the moment we get to Mount Rainier and head back to Seattle. You have two days off, what's the rush? Your patients are all stable."

"For now," Emily mumbled.

"They're in good hands. You lectured me earlier on about professional relationships. Don't you trust your colleagues to take care of your post-ops?"

"Yes," she said through gritted teeth. She liked control and order. Control and order calmed her and the world made sense then.

"That doesn't sound very convincing."

"I have a particular way of doing things," she said in exasperation.

"You don't take time off, do you?"

Emily rolled her eyes. "Fine. I don't. Work is my life."

"It shouldn't be."

"And you're telling me that work isn't your life? You, who won't settle down anywhere?"

"Hey, I do take my days off and I enjoy my time. When I'm in a new place I go and see the sights. Just like I'm doing now."

Emily couldn't help but wonder if he had a different woman in each city. One he took out on dates and wined and dined. That little green-eyed monster who shouldn't care about these things reared its ugly head.

"Okay," she finally said. "Let's stop and look at the pioneer museum. I loved *Little House on the Prairie* when I was a kid, so I think that it would be interesting to see what Ohop Bob's Pioneer Museum is like."

"You're serious?" he asked, and he looked slightly horrified at the prospect.

"You offered," she teased.

"I seriously didn't think you would take me up on it."

She laughed. "Well, I am. Let's go."

"Maybe it'll be closed," he muttered.

She couldn't help but chuckle. "It'll be fun!"

He shot her a look of disbelief and followed the signs off the highway to the museum. There was no one else there and it looked like the museum had just opened.

"Well, this is the town of Eatonville," Emily remarked as they got out of the SUV. "Perhaps Ohop Bob was an old name?"

"Let's hope so," Ryan said under his breath. "Because that's a very interesting name."

"Every state has a weird name."

"What's Utah's?"

"There are a few. Mostly people think they're odd because they're Biblical names or names of Mormon prophets. I always thought La Verkin was odd, but that might've been a misunderstanding between the locals of the area and the trappers mapping the territory. What's Wyoming's?"

"Probably Jay Em. It was named after a rancher."

"And you're making fun of Ohop Bob?" she teased.

"True." He rubbed the back of his neck. "I should probably shut up now."

"Good idea."

They walked into the museum together and Emily offered to pay the admission since Ryan was doing the driving and had packed the picnic lunch. They wandered around the museum and looked at the exhibits of frontier life in Washington State.

"Oh, look at this old furniture!" She gasped excitedly.

"You really like this, huh?" he asked, not so excited about it.

"I do."

She loved everything to do with early settlers. She loved the *Little House* books. For about five years of her life she had been obsessed with everything to do with pioneer life and the *Little House* books.

Her dream had always been to go on a road trip to see the sites where the Ingalls had traveled. She'd loved the books so much she'd wanted to wear a bonnet and pinafore every day.

Until the other kids had made fun of her for liking something so wholesome, so childish.

"No…uh. It's okay." She walked away, embarrassed.

"Hey, you okay?" Ryan asked, catching up.

"I don't mean to bore you."

"You like this stuff."

"And you clearly don't."

"So?" he asked.

"Ryan, I loved this so much as a kid. I was made fun of. I didn't have many friends...the books were my friends."

His expression softened. "Don't be ashamed. I didn't have many friends growing up either."

She found that hard to believe. "Seriously?"

"I grew up on a ranch that wasn't very successful. My clothes were from the thrift store. I was the poor kid in town."

"I was the kid with autism." And her voice shook when she admitted that.

His eyes widened. "What?"

"I have a very mild and high-functioning form of Asperger's. I'm borderline on the spectrum. As a kid..." She struggled to say the right words. "Even as an adult... it's hard."

She couldn't look at him. Couldn't take his rejection.

He placed his hand under chin and tilted her head up so she was looking at him. Tears stung her eyes. She hated feeling vulnerable to him, to anyone. But instead of rejection and pity, there was something close to admiration in his eyes. It surprised her.

"Don't be ashamed," he said gently. "Never be ashamed about how hard you've worked, about how you view the world. You're amazing!"

She smiled. "Thank you."

He nodded. "Now, how about you tell me about this old whatchamacallit here?"

She chuckled as he pointed at an old payphone that the museum hadn't bothered to remove.

"You mean the payphone?"

He did a double take and laughed. "It's dusty in here. I'm going to blame the dust for my mistake."

"Sure. It's the dust's fault," she teased.

Ohop Bob dealt with lumber, so a lot of the old way of life focused on that. Emily could tell that Ryan was completely bored out of his mind, but she appreciated his effort. Especially after he'd said those things to her about her admission to him. Not many had been that supportive.

Usually she got "Well you don't look like you have autism". That was one she never knew how to take. Was there a look she was unaware of? So it was nice he'd told her not to be ashamed and to hold her head up high.

After they wandered around for about forty minutes, she put him out of his misery and suggested they continue on their way.

She could tell he was relieved.

They weren't far from the national park's Longmire Gate and even though she'd really wanted to stay in Seattle and do research, she was actually starting to relax and enjoy the drive.

Maybe this won't be so bad?

And the thought of relaxing around him was scaring her. Even though he said the right things, she was afraid of letting her guard down too much.

This was not what she had planned at all when she'd learned he was coming to Seattle but, then again, since when did plans for her personal life ever go smoothly?

Ryan wished the conversation about his father had never come up, but he had been the one to start it and that had been by accident. Being around Emily stirred up a lot of emotions he wasn't sure that he was completely ready to deal with.

Emotions about his parents and his childhood. The loss of his child. The reason he never stayed settled, though he secretly wanted to settle down and just stay put for a while. He was getting tired.

If you settle somewhere, what happened with Morgan will happen again, and you know it. You can't stay put. Just like your father.

He wasn't worthy enough to be a father.

Who says?

He shook that thought away and stopped in front of the Valor Monument, which was dedicated to those who'd died while serving the park. Rangers who had died in the line of duty, trying to save people who were injured and hurt.

It was an impressive sculpture.

Emily was wandering a few feet away, her hands in the pockets of her hoodie, and when she turned to the side he couldn't help but stare at the round swell where his baby was.

His baby.

He wanted a family. He wanted his child and to settle down, but he was too afraid that his presence in their lives would do more harm than good. Morgan had certainly thought so.

Of course, she hadn't wanted the baby.

Emily seemed to want the baby. Or at least she said she did. Morgan had never given him the choice. He'd found out after she'd got rid of the baby.

Emily wanted the baby.

When she wasn't watching he could see her touch her

belly often and there was always this gentle, secret smile on her face. It made his pulse quicken and he longed to take her in his arms and hold them both close.

As if she knew he was watching her, she turned back and looked at him. She smiled at him, so sweetly.

God, she was beautiful.

Emily took his breath away.

She deserved so much better than him. She was intelligent, feisty and brilliant. She didn't back down and he totally respected her for that. And to learn she'd overcome so much to get where she was endeared her to him even more. He admired her for that.

It's what made her a good surgeon.

And she deserved so much better than him. It was just that when he was around her, he didn't feel as lonely. She made him laugh. He looked forward to seeing her and he enjoyed spending time with her, and he was selfish and wanted to continue this. He wanted to be selfish and keep her all to himself, even if he didn't deserve to have her.

He just wanted to enjoy every moment with her until he left.

"What're you looking at?" she asked as she came over to where he was standing.

"The Monument of Valor. Rangers who died in the line of duty, trying to save people."

"Wow, that's wonderful."

"It is," Ryan said. "We don't give police officers, soldiers…those on the front lines, the first responders enough credit. We as surgeons get all the glory, but these people put their lives on the line every day and are never recognized."

She nodded. "My dad was a police officer in Salt Lake City."

"Was he?"

"He's retired now. I remember every night he came home late, Mom would send us all to bed and pace. She wouldn't go to bed until he came home safe. I didn't get it until I was an adult and in relationships, but even then I don't know… I don't know if I've ever loved someone that much."

"No?"

"Have you?"

Yes.

"No."

He'd cared about Morgan, but had she cared about him? He didn't think so, because if she'd loved him she wouldn't have done what she had. He did respect her choice, but it had still crushed him.

It'd broken his heart.

And Morgan hadn't seemed to care.

"The trail is this way," Ryan said, clearing his voice and pointing in the direction they were supposed to go. "Want to have a quick—?"

His words were cut off by the loud blare of a siren and the ground began to quake.

"Oh, my God!" Emily cried out, and she reached out to him, wrapping her arms around him. He held her close as what sounded like a freight train echoed through the valley, while the siren continued to blare.

They were far enough above the river bed. They were safe, but still his heart was racing as he held Emily close, her body trembling against him.

It felt like an eternity before the shaking subsided and the sirens finally stopped blaring. There was a lahar somewhere. In the late spring, with melt water running and seismic activity, he wasn't surprised that it had happened.

Even though he'd sworn to Emily he didn't think it could happen.

If they hadn't stopped at that pioneer museum, they might've been on a trail, caught up in it, which was a scary thought indeed.

There was a flurry of activity and several rangers came rushing by. One stopped in front of them.

"You okay?" the ranger asked.

"We're fine," Ryan said.

Emily was still clinging to him, but not as tightly as she had before.

"I'm good," Emily said. "What happened?"

"A lahar. We're headed down the trail to check for injuries. There was a school group down there."

"I'm a pediatric surgeon," Emily said. "I can help." And suddenly what overwhelmed her had dissipated and she was putting the care of injured people first. It was admirable.

"Me too. I'm a surgeon." Although Ryan didn't really want Emily to go down the trail where the lahar had just happened. Not in her condition. But if there were kids down there, they had to help.

"Great," the ranger said. "We can use all the help we can get. Follow me and I'll take you in my truck."

Ryan and Emily followed the ranger to his truck. Ryan helped Emily up and climbed in beside her. It was a bit squished, but it was fine. He just hoped that no kids were injured.

The ride down the trail was bumpy and rough. It took over half an hour to get down to where the trapped school class was gathered. It looked like the teachers had managed to get the kids above the river bed to a safe area, the problem was that the washout had surrounded them on all sides.

They were stuck.

Rangers were slowly getting a kid across to safety. At least they weren't young children. They looked to be pre-teens. Just from this side he could tell there were some scrapes and what looked to be minor injuries.

The ranger they were riding with parked the truck.

"You folks stay here and we'll bring the kids up to you." The ranger headed down toward where the lahar had washed out the trail.

The place was littered with mud and fallen trees and though it looked stable to cross, Ryan knew it wasn't.

They were safe where the ranger had told them to stay, but he still didn't like Emily this close to the action.

"Maybe you should wait in the truck," Ryan suggested.

"I'm good. We're safe here." She crossed her arms and watched the progress of the rescue.

Ryan stood next to her and put his arm around her. She didn't shy away; her body still trembling from the adrenaline.

"You okay?" he asked.

"Not completely, but if I focus on the kids and the rescue I will be." She smiled up at him. "Saving lives is more important than the anxiety and sensory overload I'm experiencing right now. It's how I deal with it."

He nodded. "Good plan."

He'd never been so terrified in his life.

And it wasn't because he was fearing for his own life. He was terrified about losing her and that was something unexpected and unwelcome.

He wasn't sure he had enough of his heart left to deal with the idea that he could lose Emily or the baby.

Or both of them.

Emily finished bandaging up the last of the kids who had been rescued off the trail after the lahar had come sweeping down the river bed.

Thankfully no one was seriously hurt.

The kids were being taken to the hospital, but at least everyone was stable.

"It was so scary," Jessica said as Emily cleaned out her wound and wrapped it.

"I bet. I was scared when those sirens went off." She finished wrapping the wound. "I forgot Rainier was a volcano. And this is my first time experiencing a lahar."

Jessica giggled. "You're not from Washington State?"

"No. Utah. We have mountains but not volcanoes." Emily stood up. "You're ready to go in the ambulance and I heard from one of the rangers that your parents are waiting for you at the hospital."

"Good," Jessica said, relieved.

Emily left so that the paramedics could help the girl into one of the ambulances. Ryan was finishing up and helping with one of the rangers who had slipped and fallen while doing the rescue. They had to make sure that the ranger's spine was stable for the transfer.

Emily appreciated that he was there and that he'd held her when she'd been terrified and overwhelmed. She'd never experienced a lahar before. It had been terrifying and she had never before felt as helpless and vulnerable as at that moment, clinging to Ryan.

She hated that Ryan had seen her like that.

She never let anyone see her like that and she was

glad she'd told Ryan. She was glad that he was there. Of course, she would never been here if it hadn't been for his bright idea to come to the park.

Ryan finished with his patient as another ambulance came and loaded the injured ranger. Ryan walked over to her.

"You okay?" he asked.

"I'm fine. Tired, but fine."

He nodded. "Perhaps it was a bad idea to come today."

She laughed. "You think? How is the ranger?"

"He's fine. Nothing broken, but there could be some bruising or a hematoma. They won't know until they get an MRI of his spine. He's wiggling his toes well and he has a slight concussion. They'll take good care of him in the hospital."

"Are you ready to go?"

Ryan nodded. "We just have to find a ranger to drive us back up to the main lodge at Longmire."

"I can take you," a paramedic said. "I don't have anyone in my rig."

"That would be great," Emily said.

They followed the paramedic to his rig and Ryan helped her up in the back. The paramedic closed the doors and then climbed in next to his partner. Riding in the back of the ambulance was a little bit bumpier than the ranger's pickup truck had been.

Ryan placed his arm around her to help steady her, but she shimmied away, not saying anything, and he didn't ask her why.

No matter how hard she tried, she just couldn't seem to keep her distance from him. This was not like her at all and she was annoyed with herself. She'd worked hard her whole life not to depend on anyone so she could make a life for herself. Yet she was glad Ryan was here. He calmed her.

The ambulance stopped and the paramedic opened the doors.

"Thank you for your help again, doctors. We appreciated it."

"You're welcome," Emily said.

The paramedic closed up the doors to the rig and within a few moments the ambulance drove away toward the main gates of the park. It was quiet at the main Longmire lodge. It was almost three in the afternoon and the only sound were those of birds, the whispering of the pine trees and the silent tension that seemed to have formed between the two of them in that short ambulance ride.

"Are you hungry?" Ryan asked.

"Starving," Emily admitted.

"We're really overdue for lunch. I was planning on taking the hike down the trail to have lunch by the river, but I think we'll just stick around here."

"That's a good plan." She followed him to his SUV and he pulled out a cooler from the back hatch, as well as a blanket.

They didn't walk far and found a sunny spot not far from the parking lot, but where they could still see Mount Rainier and the valley well enough. The park was quiet, because not all the trails were completely open yet and the rangers had closed off the trail they had just been down until the aftermath of the lahar could be dealt with.

Ryan laid out the blanket and Emily sat down and began to pull things out of the cooler. He sat down next to her.

"I'm sorry that I grabbed you when the ground started

shaking," she said. "I think that made it sort of awkward between us."

"I didn't mind that you grabbed me, Emily."

Warmth flooded her cheeks and she looked up at him. He was serious, he hadn't minded, but something had changed and she didn't know what.

"Are you mad that I moved away from you in the back of the rig?" she asked.

He shook his head. "No. I'm not mad. I don't want to overwhelm you. I want to help you while I'm here, as much as I can."

"Is that what you want or what you feel obligated to do?"

He sighed and looked straight ahead. "I want a family, but I also don't know if I can stay settled. My career is important."

"You're not used to that, staying in one place."

"Right. I do like traveling... My dad could never stay in one place either. Maybe I'm just like him. Maybe..." He trailed off and she sensed that there was something more, only he didn't say. "I don't want to hurt you, Emily. I never wanted that and if I had known you were pregnant..."

"You wouldn't have stayed. You had important work."

"I want to be there for you and the baby," he said seriously. "That's my baby too and I'm here right now and I want to help."

Emily really wanted to believe him. He was so earnest, but she knew he couldn't stay. Still, he had a right to his child.

"You can be as involved as you like."

He nodded. "Thank you."

She reached out and took his hand. "My appointment with Dr. Samuel is in a couple of days. Come to it."

"I will."

"You promise?" she asked.

"I promise." He handed her a bottle of water. "You don't trust me, though, and that's okay. We barely know each other."

"I don't trust many people," she said. "I used to, but then they took advantage because I didn't understand things like lying and sarcasm."

"What happened?" he asked.

Emily sighed. She hated talking about Robert. It was embarrassing to her that she had fallen in love with a man who couldn't handle her success, a man who'd cheated on her, belittled her. She just couldn't see it, and he'd lied to her. She mentally kicked herself over and over again for allowing a man like that into her life for so long.

She'd been a fool.

And when her parents found out she was pregnant after a one-night stand, they were thrilled that she was keeping the baby and were happy to have a grandchild, but they weren't exactly thrilled that she seemed to have fallen into the same trap as she had with Robert. They worried she wasn't able to take care of herself. They worried about her being independent and out of state. They worried she was being manipulated and taken advantage of.

That she'd fallen for a smooth operator. Although the more she got to know Ryan she was realizing that wasn't the case.

Ryan just couldn't settle down.

Still, all her mistakes weighed heavily on her. And

her mom worried she couldn't handle a child who might have autism. That it would be too much for her, too overwhelming for her. Emily worried about that too, but she wasn't going to go running back home. She was capable of living on her own. She could do this.

"I was in a relationship with a man who lied to me, who cheated on me. I was in love with someone who didn't deserve my love and I swore I would never fall for another surgeon again. I had been doing fine for five years."

Ryan smiled, his eyes twinkling. "Until you met me."

"Yes, until I met you and we had that ill-fated night in Las Vegas." She sighed. "I don't regret that night. I just never wanted to get involved with another surgeon ever again, but I don't regret that night."

"So that's why you don't trust me."

"I'm sorry. It's hard for me to trust."

"No, don't be sorry. I get it, but I will say this—you can trust me. I may not be settled, but when it comes to our baby, I won't let you down."

It was sweet that he'd said that and she wanted to believe him. She just wasn't sure that she could. Emily leaned over and touched his face.

Maybe give him the benefit of the doubt?

He touched her cheek, his fingers brushing against her skin. She closed her eyes and reveled in the feeling of his touch. She couldn't help but think of the last time he'd touched her like this and how fast she'd fallen into his arms.

She'd missed this. Even though she hadn't wanted to miss this, she did. She'd missed this moment of intimacy and connection, but it scared her too.

"I would never do anything to hurt you or the baby," he whispered.

"I know."

And then before she knew what was happening she was leaning closer to him and getting lost in the feelings he was stirring in her. Feelings that she tried so hard to control, to keep locked away, but when she was with him he brought down all her barriers.

She was exposed and vulnerable to him.

She closed her eyes as he kissed her, gently, but full of a controlled longing that she understood all too well. It made her pulse quicken, her blood heat as she melted into a kiss that burned through her body like an untamed wildfire.

And that's what Ryan had always brought out in her. Uncontrolled need.

Emily pushed him away and it took her a moment to catch her breath.

"It's a long drive and I think we should head back to Seattle," she said finally.

Ryan nodded. "You're right. Finish your lunch and I'll clean up."

He got up and picked up some garbage to throw out.

Emily took a deep breath and tried to calm the erratic beat of her heart. She was playing a dangerous game with her heart and she wasn't sure she would survive it.

And she wasn't sure she wanted to.

CHAPTER NINE

IT HAD BEEN a couple days since Emily had seen Ryan.
Since they'd kissed at Mount Rainier National Park. It
had been a quiet ride home and she'd fallen asleep before they'd reached the interstate.

She just remembered waking up when Ryan had
pulled up in front of her apartment. He'd helped her out
of his SUV and escorted her up to her apartment, but he
hadn't come in. Just kissed her on top of the head and
said goodnight.

Emily was still trying to process everything that had
happened that day and how she felt about it. She was so
confused.

There was a part of her that was telling her not to trust
Ryan, because she couldn't trust a man who wouldn't settle down and he was a surgeon. It was a double whammy,
but then he looked at her and spoke so kindly to her.

Robert had never spoken that way to her. And as she
looked back to that disastrous relationship she was so
mad at herself for thinking that it had been good when
she'd been in it. It was clear to her now that it hadn't
been.

It never had been.

She was just so afraid of getting hurt again, but Ryan

was so different and she knew, deep down, that he would never hurt her or the baby.

Maybe give him a chance?

The idea of giving him a chance was scary.

There was a page and she looked down to see that Ryan was paging her and that he needed her urgently down in Pathology.

Her stomach twisted, because if he was in Pathology that could only mean one thing—Raquel's results were in.

Please, don't be bad. Please, don't be bad.

She logged off the computer and headed out of her office. She made her way through the halls and found Ryan just outside the pathology area. He was leaning against the wall and had his head in his hand.

"I'm here," she said. "Is that Raquel's report?"

He handed it to her. "Malignant. She has cancer. I'm going to send her to CT to see if it's spread."

Emily nodded. "That's a good idea."

"I was hoping you could come with me to tell them the news. She is your patient and if there are metastases in her body, we can both tackle the surgeries to get rid of them."

"Okay."

Ryan scrubbed a hand over his face. "Giving news about cancer is never easy, but with kids it sucks. I much prefer working on adults."

She touched his arm. "It's okay. Kids are resilient. More resilient than adults. We'll tackle this together. If there are no other mets in her body, are you planning on taking out the tumor?"

He nodded. "Yes, right now it's on the smaller side. If it gets any bigger I won't be able to successfully resect it and leave good margins. The sooner we get this done the better."

"Okay. Let's go tell Raquel's mother together. We'll let Raquel's mother break the news to her daughter and we'll be there for them. That's all we can do."

They walked side by side up to Raquel's room.

Raquel was sleeping and her mother, Vanessa, was sitting by her bedside, reading a book. Emily's heart ached with the news she had to deliver to her. She could feel tears welling up in her eyes and she had to maintain her composure.

"Vanessa, can Dr. Gary and I speak with you?"

Vanessa nodded and snuck away from Raquel's bedside.

"Let's go into the lounge area here." And the moment Emily suggested that she could see the blood drain from Vanessa's face. Ryan placed his hand on Vanessa's back gently for reassurance. Emily waited until they were all in the room and Vanessa was seated. She shut the door and that's when Vanessa began to cry.

"It's malignant. Isn't it?" Vanessa asked.

Ryan took Vanessa's hand. "It is. I'm sorry."

Vanessa nodded and Emily handed her a tissue and took a seat next to her. Emily was trying to fight back the urge to cry. She had to get hold of her emotions.

She had better control than this.

"So, what happens now?"

"We're going to take Raquel for a CT scan, to make sure that the cancer hasn't spread, then we can come up with a course of treatment," Emily said.

"Either way, I want to do surgery to resect the tumor," Ryan added. "I want to operate before it gets too large and her seizures get worse and she loses more function."

Vanessa nodded. "This is a lot to take in. I'm a single mom and I'm missing so much work and the cost…"

"You let me worry about that," Ryan said. "I have pro bono funds still available. I can't speak for SMFPC."

"Don't worry about that," Emily assured her. "The most important thing is Raquel and her well-being. I'm going to have my intern, Dr. Teal, take Raquel for a CT scan stat and then Dr. Gary will be able to assess and determine the best course of action for surgery. I will have our pediatric oncology team contact you."

Vanessa nodded and rubbed her temple. "It's a lot to take in. Raquel is all I have in this world…"

A lump formed in Emily's throat. She found it hard to speak. "You won't lose her. Kids are resilient and we're going to do everything in our power to make sure you two are together for a long time. The cancer is aggressive and as soon as we get the scan done we can stage it and go from there."

Vanessa nodded. "Thank you, doctors. Thank you for being there that night and thank you for helping us now."

Ryan stood when Vanessa got up and left.

"I'll go with her and answer Raquel's questions," Ryan said.

"I'll get Dr. Teal to book that CT scan." And then Emily couldn't help but shed a tear. She covered her mouth and tried to hold back the sobs.

"Hey," Ryan said gently. He knelt down in front of her and place his hands on her knees in a comforting gesture. "What's wrong?"

"I don't know," she sniffled. "Do you know how many kids I've had to operate on that had cancer? Too many, and none of them affected me like this is affecting me. It has to be the pregnancy. I usually don't give in to the emotions when I'm overwhelmed, but that was hard. I couldn't help it."

"It could be hormones. This is affecting me as well, but that's because I don't always work with kids and I hate to see any kid have cancer. You're strong, Emily. You see it all the time and you save lives. You're stronger than me."

Emily wiped her eyes. "Thank you for being so kind."

He tipped her chin. "It's not being kind, stating fact."

"Go help Raquel."

"Are you going to be okay?"

She nodded. "Yes. I'll be fine."

"Okay." Ryan stood and left the room.

Emily took a deep, calming breath. She had to get it together. This was not like her at all. She was losing control and that was not acceptable to her. When she stood up she felt dizzy. Really light-headed.

It took her a few moments before she felt well enough to leave the room. She left the small lounge and paged Dr. Teal. She took a seat the nurses' station and waited for Dr. Teal to arrive, which she did a few minutes later.

"You paged, Dr. West?" Amanda asked.

"I need you to take the patient in 607 down for a CT scan stat. Her biopsy can back positive for cancer."

Amanda's face fell. "Of course, Dr. West."

When Dr. Teal left, Emily stood up too quickly and again felt the room spinning.

"Dr. West?" she heard someone say, only she couldn't respond as a strange sensation washed over her and she felt her knees give out before the world went black.

"So I'm going to lose my hair, then?" Raquel asked him.

"Chemo and radiation does do that. There's no getting around that, but before the chemo does that I'll have to shave part of your head anyway to get at the tumor."

Raquel sighed and glanced at her mom. "Well, I guess that's okay."

Ryan sat down next to Raquel. "I can see that it's not okay. So, because I have to shave your head, you get to shave mine."

"Dr. Gary, that's not necessary," Vanessa said.

Raquel's eyes lit up. "Really? Can I shave it in a strange pattern?"

"No. I do draw the line at racing stripes or some weird cartoon. You can give me a buzz cut, like they do in the army."

Raquel nodded. "Okay, Dr. Gary. That's a deal!"

Ryan smiled. "I thought that might cheer you up."

There was a knock at the door and Dr. Teal was there. "Dr. Gary, we're here to take Raquel down to CT."

Ryan nodded and stood up. "I'll see you later. Dr. Teal, as soon as the images are up I want to be paged."

"Yes, of course, Dr. Gary."

He left the room. Dr. Teal could handle taking Raquel down for a CT scan. He was hoping that the malignancy hadn't spread. Usually in adults primary brain tumors were rare, they usually came from another adenocarcinoma like lung cancer, but in kids it was common to have a primary brain tumor.

So he was hoping that's all Raquel had.

Something that he could resect out and she'd have minimal chemo and radiation along with immunotherapy, and she'd be on her way to recovery.

He hoped it was as simple as that.

As soon as he walked into the hallway a nurse rushed over to him.

"Dr. Gary, we've been looking for you!"

Ryan was confused. "Me? Is Jason okay?" That was the only other patient besides Raquel that he currently had at this hospital until the conjoined twins were born and were ready to be separated.

"Jason is fine," the nurse said. "Dr. West is with Dr. Samuel in the maternity wing. She fainted."

Ryan didn't stay to hear any more. He turned around quickly and ran as fast as he could toward the other side of SMFPC, to the wing where pregnant mothers came to deliver their children or were waiting to deliver their children.

His blood was pounding in his ears as he ran as fast as his legs could carry him, dodging people as he crossed the covered walkway that connected the two wings. It didn't take him long to find Dr. Samuel's office.

A nurse in the maternity wing knew who he was looking for and shouted out the room number as he ran past.

He didn't even knock, just burst into the room.

Emily looked pale and she was lying on a table with her eyes closed. There was a little cut on her head that had been closed with Steri-Strips.

"Em?" he said, as he crouched down next to the bed.

"Ryan?" she asked. "How did you know I was here?"

"A nurse told me. I came as soon as I found out. Are you okay? Is the baby okay?"

"She's fine," Dr. Samuel said, coming into the room. "She had a drop in blood sugar, so I want to do a glucose tolerance test and check for gestational diabetes. She also hit her head, but she's not exhibiting any signs of concussion."

"And the baby?" Ryan asked, unable to really process

anything that the doctor was saying. He was just terrified that the baby was gone. That he'd lost another child.

"The baby is fine," Dr. Samuel said. "Do you want to hear the heart beat?"

"Yes," Ryan said.

Dr. Samuel squeezed some more ultrasound jelly on Emily's belly and used the Doppler. There was a lot of static at first, whooshing noises that he knew was Emily's blood, and then there it was. A little heart, beating so fast.

The baby's heart.

"Strong heartbeat," Dr. Samuel said, smiling.

Ryan squeezed Emily's hand and just listened in disbelief. It was amazing, it was strong and it was his child's.

"I want you to go home for the rest of the day, Emily. Rest. Nothing to eat or drink after midnight and then come back first thing in the morning and I'll do your glucose tolerance test."

"Okay, Alex," Emily said demurely.

"Dr. Gary, do you think you can take Emily home?"

Emily's eyes widened. "He has patients."

"I can take her home," Ryan stated firmly.

"Ryan, you have Raquel…"

"She's going through a CT scan right now and Dr. Teal can email me the scans. I can't do the surgery until tomorrow anyway. I can take you home and take care of you tonight. You hit your head and your blood sugar dropped. I'm not letting you out of my sight."

Emily sighed and took the towel Dr. Samuel handed her to wipe the ultrasound jelly off her abdomen.

Ryan helped her sit up.

"You wait here and I'm going to get your things in the lounge and pull my car around to this side of the hospital."

"It's no big deal…" Emily tried to argue.

"Listen to him and do what he says," Dr. Samuel said, before leaving the room.

Emily rolled her eyes.

"Stay put!" Ryan ordered, and then smiled.

"Fine." Emily crossed her arms, but he could see a smile tugging at the corners of her mouth.

Ryan left the exam room and when he closed the door he leaned against it and let out the breath he hadn't known he'd been holding. He scrubbed a hand over his face and then headed back to the other side of the hospital.

He had been so worried that something had happened to Emily or the baby.

It was the same kind of terror he'd felt when they had been at Mount Rainier National Park and the geohazard siren had gone off, right before the lahar had hit.

The thought of losing either one of them made him feel sick to his stomach and it also scared him. The worry was too much and he wasn't sure he could let his heart be on the line. He wasn't sure he could handle the heartache again.

Just like he wasn't sure that he knew how to be a father.

And he hated himself for his fear, his hurt and uncertainty.

Right now, though, he would try and do his best for Emily and the baby.

He wouldn't walk away like his father had.

At least not yet.

* * *

Emily was propped up in bed.

At least she had a television in her room or she'd go bonkers, because ever since Ryan had brought her home, he'd been hovering and not letting her take one step out of bed.

"I'm not on bed rest, you know!" she shouted so that Ryan, who was in the kitchen, could hear her. "He just said to go home for the night and rest."

"And where do you rest?" Ryan asked.

Emily rolled her eyes. "In bed."

"Right." He handed her a cup of tea. "I'm going to order in dinner. Would you like anything in particular?"

"Chinese food would be great."

"Isn't that a tad clichéd for a pregnancy?"

She glared at him and took a sip of her decaf tea.

"All right, all right. Just stay put and we'll rent a movie online or something."

"Don't you need to go back to the hospital?"

"I'm waiting for Dr. Teal to email me the scans and then I'll go back and decide how to proceed, but the surgery really can't be done until tomorrow. Raquel had lunch and a snack. I'll bring you to the hospital tomorrow for your glucose tolerance test and then I'll do the surgery."

"What about your other patient?"

"Jason?" Ryan asked.

"Yes."

"He's stable and in good hands in his room." That was all he said about Jason, which meant he hadn't regained any control yet. She could tell that it was weighing heavily on Ryan, which was why he was probably overcompensating with her.

Ryan left the room to place the order and Emily leaned back, setting her tea on the nightstand. She was still feeling a bit woozy and her head was hurting from when it'd hit the floor. She touched it gingerly and winced.

"Don't poke it," Ryan said, coming back into the room.

"I'm not."

"You are." He sat down on the edge of the bed and checked his phone. "The food should be here in forty minutes."

"Good. Any word?"

He shook his head. "Nothing."

Emily reached over and picked up her tablet. She opened up the MRI scan that had been done of Janet. Ryan hadn't seen the scans of the babies.

"Take a look at that. Since you're not going to let me out of bed and you're planning to stick around, perhaps we can talk about this."

Ryan picked up the table and then kicked off his shoes, scooting back so he was sitting upright next to her.

"That's a lot of nerves bundled together."

"Do you think you'll be able to separate them without paralyzing them?" she asked.

"I believe so." Ryan flipped through the images. "I won't really know until I get in there and start to separate them. I'll have nerve monitors on them. I want to make sure I don't paralyze them and I won't know that until I go in. The hardest job will be flipping them to do that."

"It's like a puzzle," Emily said, leaning over him. "Every case of conjoined twins is different."

"Well, if they were all the same it wouldn't be such a problem."

"I wish that were the case." Emily picked up her tea and took another sip. "How did Raquel take the news?"

"She was scared," Ryan said, setting down the tablet. "I think I made her happy when I told her what she could do to me."

"What?" Emily asked, confused. "What're you talking about?"

"Since I have to shave her head to resect the tumor, she gets to shave mine."

Emily was glad she hadn't taken a sip of tea just then because she would've spit it out all over him. "You promised a ten-year-old child that she could shave your head?"

"Well, a buzz cut. She wanted to add racing stripes, but I vetoed that."

Emily cocked an eyebrow. "You're taking your patient care a little too seriously."

"It made her happy."

She smiled. He was so good with kids. She just hoped that he'd be around for their baby. He'd be a good father.

And that was the first time she'd thought of the baby as their baby.

It had always been her baby from the get-go and she couldn't help but wonder when that change in her mind had come, but it had.

"So no racing stripes, eh?" she teased, and then she reached out and ran her fingers through his brown hair. "I'm not sure how you're going to look with a buzz cut. You have really great hair."

"I've had buzz cuts before. You just didn't know me when I did." He pulled out his phone and pulled up an old photograph and showed her. "See, it's my high-school yearbook photo. I had a buzz cut then."

Emily chuckled. He was so skinny and awkward and young in the image.

"Why do you have an old picture of yourself on your phone?"

"To remind me how far I've come."

"And you need to be reminded?" she asked.

"Some days."

An awkward silence fell between them, just like it had after they'd shared that kiss at Mount Rainier National Park. He pocketed his phone just as the buzzer to her apartment sounded.

"Hopefully that's the food." Ryan got up and headed to the front door.

Emily lay back and closed her eyes. She wished she could just come right out and ask him about his future plans. She wished that she could trust him.

She wished for a lot of things but she wasn't sure that she was ever going to get them.

They ate Chinese food in her room. Ryan had managed to find a breakfast tray so that Emily wouldn't be tempted to get out of bed because she'd been afraid of making a mess in her bed, which was what she had said when he'd first brought the bag of Chinese take-away into her room.

She'd ranted on about expensive cotton sheets and had said she felt well enough to sit at the dining-room table, but he was having none of that. She'd hit her head and even though she had been cleared of a concussion, he hadn't wanted to take any chances. She'd hit her head hard enough that it had bled and they'd needed to put Steri-Strips on it.

Eventually he'd won out by telling her he was the

neurosurgeon and she should listen to him. He had compromised and found an old breakfast tray in the back of her pantry, covered in dust. He'd washed it off and brought her food.

He brought in a chair and sat next to her bed, because the last thing he wanted to do was make her angry about ruining her sheets. Even though he really wanted to sit next to her. Her bed was much more comfortable than the hotel's bed he was sleeping in.

Definitely better than her couch, which was where he'd slept the first night he'd been in Seattle. They watched an old comedy movie from the 1980s that had been popular when they'd been much younger, but now was just completely corny, though Emily admitted she still loved it, and that just made him fall for her even more.

Eventually, she drifted off to sleep and Ryan cleared away all the food and got her a glass of water for her bedside.

She looked so peaceful, sleeping.

He wished he could stay, but the CT scan results were in and he couldn't pull them up on his phone. He would have to go into the hospital to check them out or get her to tell him the passcode for her tablet.

"Emily," he whispered.

"Yes?" she asked groggily. "Have the results come in?"

"Yes, but I can't pull them up on my phone. Sorry to wake you but I need you to unlock your tablet so I can take a look. Unless you want me to go to the hospital."

Emily sat up and picked up her tablet. She unlocked it. "I want to know the results too."

"Fair enough." Ryan logged into his email and opened

up the scans. He studied them thoroughly and let out a sigh of relief. "No mets anywhere else, which means this malignancy is a stage two at the most."

"That's great," Emily said, stifling a yawn. "I'm really glad to hear it."

Ryan pulled out his phone to call Dr. Teal. He wanted an operating room booked for tomorrow morning and he wanted Dr. Teal, who was on call, to prep Raquel for surgery.

"Hi, Dr. Teal, it's Dr. Gary. I need you to prep Raquel for surgery and book an operating room for tomorrow morning. As early as you can. Thank you."

Ryan hung up the phone. "Who do you think the best pediatric oncologist in SMFPC is?"

"Dr. Ramses. She's the best."

"I'll make a referral to her." Ryan sent off the scans and the chart to Dr. Ramses electronically and almost immediately got a response that Dr. Ramses would see Raquel tomorrow morning before the surgery. "Dr. Ramses will see Raquel before I take her to the OR."

"You'd better get there even earlier if you're going to let Raquel shave your head," Emily said, a smile quirking her lips. She looked so tired and he felt bad for waking her.

"Do you want me to leave so you can get some rest?" he asked gently.

Not that he wanted to leave, but he really should.

"No. Stay. It's late and you have an early morning tomorrow."

"So do you."

She nodded. "I'm not looking forward to the glucose tolerance test. I'm not a fan of orange soda, especially thick, syrupy orange soda."

"That doesn't sound appealing."

"It's not. Or so I've been told by patients." She closed her eyes and drifted off to sleep again.

Ryan slipped off his shoes, which he had put back on because he'd been planning to leave and head back to the hospital. Even though he shouldn't stay, because he was just torturing himself getting more and more involved with her, he wanted to stay. Emily had asked him to stay.

She found comfort in his presence.

You're going to break her heart when you leave.

And that thought made him feel ill.

Unless he stayed. He could focus on pediatric neuro-surgery. He was versed in both. He liked Seattle and if he stayed here then he could be close to Emily and the baby. Maybe then they wouldn't have to get divorced. They could stay married and try to make it work.

He was falling for her.

He cared for her and desired her, especially after their time in Vegas, but something was changing and shifting. Emily got through all the barriers he'd set up for himself to protect his heart.

Barriers that he'd been setting for himself since his father had left him and his mom. Barriers that he'd been putting in place since his mother had disowned him be-cause he hadn't wanted to follow the path that she'd wanted him to follow. He hadn't wanted to stay on the land, like his father hadn't wanted to stay. He had left, just like his dad.

Barriers that had been put in place when Morgan had terminated her pregnancy.

All those barriers he'd put in place to protect his heart. Only Emily was wiggling her way through and he wasn't sure if he had what it took to give her the life she deserved. He wasn't even sure that he knew how to love.

And he wasn't sure that he'd be a good father. He was so like his dad.

He'd met up with his father again once as an adult, before he'd met Morgan. His father had looked him up, needing medical advice, but their meeting had been brief and very awkward, and they hadn't stayed in touch. His father had only said, "I was never a good father. I didn't stick around for you or your mother. I couldn't change."

They'd parted ways and Ryan had never seen him again, and the focus of his life had been his career. How could he be a good father when he never stayed in one place long enough? When all that mattered to him was saving lives and practicing medicine?

Emily was fast asleep, and in the darkness he rolled over on his side and placed his hand on her belly. He felt the little kicks and smiled.

He couldn't walk away from this.

Not now, but he was so scared that he wasn't good enough for his child. That he would hurt this child the way his parents had hurt him.

Because you're scared means you won't.

Ryan shook that thought away because he didn't really believe it, but he had to try and believe it or this would never work. And right here and now, curled up next to Emily with his hand on her belly, feeling their baby move under his palm, he wanted it to work.

He wanted to stay.

He wanted to be here for his child. When he'd heard that heart beating it had thrilled him and scared him at the same time. Lives were always in his hands as a surgeon, but this life, this life under his hand was something completely different. It was a life that he and Emily had created.

Together.

He leaned in and put his face close to her belly, close to where his hand was resting on her belly, where he could still feel their baby kicking.

"I will try. For you. I will try," he whispered, and he meant what he said.

Every instinct was telling him to leave, that it would be better for Emily and for the baby if he left, but his heart was telling him to stay and make it work.

His heart was telling him to try and take a chance.

To take a chance on happiness, which was something he was very unfamiliar with.

CHAPTER TEN

RYAN TOOK EMILY back to Dr. Samuel's office early next morning for her glucose intolerance test, but he couldn't stay because he had to prep Raquel for surgery. Emily understood and it would be a long test. They had to test her blood at several intervals before and after the orange drink to see how her body reacted.

It would be able to tell Dr. Samuels whether or not Emily had gestational diabetes, which Ryan was hoping she didn't.

It would put a serious kink in her stamina and she might not be able to perform the conjoined twin surgery and he knew that would devastate Emily. Dr. Ruchi wanted Emily to perform the surgery because Emily was one of the best pediatric surgeons in the country with a high success rate of separations, but Dr. Ruchi was also an OB/GYN and she would understand if Emily couldn't because of pregnancy complications.

Ryan was really hoping that there were no complications.

He wasn't sure if he could handle that.

It had scared him enough when he'd found out that Emily had collapsed.

He told Emily to page him as soon as the test was

done and let him know, even if he was in surgery. One of the interns could pass him the message.

It would drive him squirrelly, not knowing.

When he got to Raquel's room, Dr. Ramses was just leaving. She had presented her treatment plan to Vanessa and Raquel.

"It's a pleasure to finally meet you, Dr. Gary," Dr. Ramses said.

"The pleasure is all mine," Ryan said, taking her hand and shaking it. "You came highly recommended by Dr. West."

Dr. Ramses smiled. "Well, I'm glad to hear that. I just went over my plan for chemotherapy, radiation and immunotherapy. Raquel won't need many doses, but I plan to start it when she's two days post-op. I want to make sure that the hormone the tumor is secreting into her blood is almost negative. Radiation will follow after her chemotherapy and once I know her brain has healed from the resection."

"That sounds like a good plan."

"I look forward to reading your post-op notes," Dr. Ramses said before she left.

Ryan found Raquel in bed, prepped and ready to go. She looked so small and scared. She turned her head when he came into the room.

"You ready for our prep?" Ryan asked he held up the electric razor.

Raquel's eyes widened. "You're serious?"

Ryan nodded. "Me first. That way you know I won't back down on my word."

Raquel sat up and Ryan sat down on the floor so she could reach his head. He knew that this was probably a foolish thing to do, but he felt so bad that this was happening to a sweet girl and he wanted to bring her joy. Give her some hope, when cancer seemed so hopeless.

He closed his eyes after the first few chunks of hair fell.

It didn't take long for Raquel to shave off his hair.

"I'm done and I swear there's no racing stripes."

Ryan got up and took the electric razor from her. "Are you ready?"

Raquel's lip trembled, but she shook her head. "If I'm going to lose it, yeah, I'm ready."

"You're very brave and strong for your age, Raquel, and that strength will get you through anything."

If only he believed in that himself for himself.

Raquel nodded and closed her eyes. Vanessa sat on the other side of the bed and held her daughter's hand as Ryan shaved off her hair. Vanessa had given him permission to shave it off as the high doses of chemo would cause it to fall out.

"There, done." Ryan set down the razor and then knelt down in front of her. "We look good."

Raquel smiled and rubbed his head.

There was a knock at the door and they looked around to see Dr. Teal and the other operating-room staff in their scrubs with a gurney.

Dr. Teal's eyes widened for a moment as she looked at him, but she kept her comments to herself.

"It's time, Dr. Gary," Dr. Teal said.

Ryan nodded and turned back to Raquel. "I'll see you in there."

"Will my mom be coming?"

"Not this time. It'll be a full house in there but don't worry, she'll be waiting for you as soon as you're out of the operating room."

Raquel nodded and Ryan left her room.

He headed straight to the operating-room floor and ignored all the pointed looks at his newly shaved head. He hadn't looked in a mirror, but he was pretty sure it was a hack job and that was okay.

Hair grew back.

He tied on a scrub cap and got ready, scrubbing in as Raquel was wheeled into the operating room. As he was scrubbing he took a moment to close his eyes and think about the next steps, and he wished that Emily was there. Her presence calmed him in the operating room, like no one else had done before, and Raquel was her patient just as much as she was his.

It had been a couple of hours since she'd started that test. He should be hearing something soon.

"They told me your shave job was awful."

Ryan turned around to see Emily standing in the doorway of the scrub room. She was dressed in scrubs and was smiling at him, her eyes twinkling.

"I would take off my scrub cap and show you, but I don't want to contaminate the field."

She chuckled. "Well, hair grows out."

"Exactly." He finished washing. "How are you feeling?"

"Good. It's not gestational diabetes. Dr. Samuel had them rush the lab so that I could get here in time. I hope there's room for me to assist?"

"There's always room. She's your patient too."

"Good." Emily began to scrub in beside him.

"So why do you think you fainted?"

"Low blood sugar. Dr. Samuel does want me to take it easier. I'm going to take some time off. My only case will be the conjoined twins, their delivery and the separation. After that is dealt with, I will take time off until the baby comes. He doesn't want me to push myself."

Ryan could have kissed Dr. Samuel right now, because he was feeling the same thing, but he knew that Emily, if she wasn't well enough, would walk away from the conjoined twins.

"I'm glad it's not diabetes. I'm glad you got the all clear," he said. "And I'm glad he's going to make you rest. You need rest."

"Me too, because I was having nightmares of me being stuck on bed rest and you hovering around and ordering in every night if he had put me on bed rest today."

Ryan laughed. "What is it that you object to? The hovering or the ordering in?"

"Both, but I honestly don't mind the hovering." She shook off her hands in the sink. "I like having you around."

Emily couldn't believe that she'd just admitted that, but it was the truth. She liked that he'd been there for her. Her parents were in Salt Lake City and she knew, deep down, that if there was a problem with her pregnancy her mother would've taken time off work and flown to Seattle to take care of her, but she was glad that Ryan was here and that she could rely on him.

Can you?

Emily shook that niggling little thought away. She didn't want to think about it. She wanted to find the positive and make herself trust him. She wanted to believe that he would be there, because the few times she'd needed him since he'd arrived in Seattle he'd been there and it was nice to be able to depend on someone, even though that independent side of her told her to only depend on herself.

It was lonely, only depending on yourself.

She had never thought she would want someone else in her life after Robert had broken her heart. She never wanted to go through that pain again. It had taken her five years and a really poor choice of a night in Las Vegas to start to change her mind, to think that maybe love like her parents had was real and obtainable after all?

Love?

She shook that thought away, because she didn't know if she was in love with him. She was so confused and she couldn't help but wonder if a lot of it was from pregnancy hormones. One thing she was certain of, she was glad she could be here with him right now.

He'd thought she'd been asleep when he'd reached out and touched her belly to feel their baby kick, when he whispered that he'd try.

Tears stung her eyes as she thought of that.

If he was willing to try, why couldn't she just bend a little and be willing to try and give this a chance?

Ryan was in the operating room and a scrub nurse had helped him on with his surgical gown and he was now standing next to Raquel, who was being positioned by the anesthesiologist. Raquel looked terrified as they draped her, but Ryan was there, comforting her.

The girl looked up at him with adoration and instantly she saw the child calm down. He may not think that he had a way with children, but he did.

And he was willing to try for their child. That meant so much.

They could talk about that later. Right now, he had

to resect the tumor out of Raquel's brain and give this child a chance at life.

Emily finished scrubbing in and walked into the operating room. Raquel glanced over at her.

"Dr. West?" she asked with hope in her voice.

"I'm here, Raquel. I thought I would help Dr. Gary out, if that's okay?"

Raquel smiled. "Okay."

Emily smiled down at her, even though Raquel couldn't see the smile from behind the surgical mask. The anesthesiologist placed a mask over Raquel's face.

"Breathe," Emily whispered to the little girl. "Deep breaths for me."

Raquel's eyes went heavy, but they didn't close. Raquel reached out for her and latched onto her arm. Emily stayed there as Raquel drifted under anesthetic, this time without the excitement phase that she had experienced the first time she'd gone under general anesthetic. Raquel's muscles relaxed and Emily moved her arm and laid it down on the table.

"She's under," the anesthesiologist said.

Emily stepped back as they taped Raquel's eyes shut and prepped the tube that would deliver the meds to keep her asleep under general anesthesia. She took her place behind the drapes where Ryan was waiting for the anesthesia to be completed so that he could start his work.

"All good, Dr. Gary," the anesthesiologist said.

"Perfect. Well, let's get this done and give this girl a fighting chance against cancer. Scalpel."

Emily had left the operating room to scrub out and fetch Raquel's mother, Vanessa, as Ryan finished closing her up. Vanessa was being taken up to the ICU because she would be out for some time yet.

The tumor had been hard to resect, but Ryan had got good margins. It just meant that it would be a harder recovery for her and Ryan wanted to make sure she got a bit more time under to allow her brain to heal.

Sleep was the best thing to allow the brain to heal.

When Emily had delivered Vanessa to the ICU, and Raquel's bedside, she went back to the operating room where Ryan was sitting, typing on a laptop. He was doing the operative report while the room was being cleaned around him.

"You did a good job," Emily said, coming into the room. They didn't have to wear their masks when the room was open.

"Thanks. I was glad to be able to leave good margins, but her recovery will be rough. As soon as I get this operating report done I'll head up to the ICU and speak with Vanessa and check on Raquel."

"Are you staying here tonight?" she asked.

He nodded. "I want to make sure she's okay, and I can check on Jason too."

Her heart sank as she thought of Jason and how that surgery weighed heavily on them both. She didn't want him to be wrong about using therapeutic hypothermia, but there was still no movement in his limbs and it was coming down to the sad realization that Jason would be a paraplegic.

"I'm going to head for home and do what my doctor ordered. I've ordered a run-through of the simulation of separation for tomorrow afternoon. Will you be able to attend that?"

He nodded. "Of course. I'll be there. Take care of yourself tonight. Get some rest and eat properly."

She laughed. "There are leftovers and I will rest."

"What time will you be coming in tomorrow?" he asked.

"Morning, probably not before nine. I want to prep the simulation lab."

He nodded. "Okay, page me when you get here. I might be asleep in one of the on-call rooms."

"I will. Try not to worry."

"I can't help that." He winked at her and then turned back to the laptop and continued typing up his operative report.

Emily sighed and then walked out of the operating room. She didn't want him to worry, but she was glad that he did seem to care enough that he was worried about her. It gave her a nice feeling, knowing that he was worried about her and the baby.

Don't get too caught up in it, that self-doubt niggled at the back of her mind, and then her doubt weasels reminded her that he hadn't responded to her right away, and even when he'd come back from his tour of duty overseas he hadn't come to find her and he'd known where she was. Especially since he had the marriage license. Her address was on there.

He could've come sooner, but he hadn't.

What if he was scared? You were scared.

She was still scared. Scared about where this was going. She was nervous that he was breaking down her walls and getting through to her, because she was sure that her heart couldn't take another blow of heartbreak, and she wasn't going to let her child feel that.

She had to be careful and even though she wanted

to walk away and put distance between her and Ryan, she couldn't.

She was falling for him.

She was falling in love.

When Emily came back to the hospital the next day to get the simulation lab ready for the conjoined twin surgery, she went up to the ICU floor to check on Raquel, but she really didn't need to do that.

Ryan was in Raquel's room, charting, and she found out from a nurse that he'd been there all night. Especially when Vanessa had needed to get something to eat or leave the room for a break. Ryan had barely left Raquel's side.

It warmed her heart.

He cared so deeply for his patients. No wonder that made him the best and it just made it easier for her to convince herself that she should give him a chance. That maybe he was worth the chance.

Ryan glanced up from his charting and saw that she was hovering in the hall. He smiled and got up to come outside.

"Good morning," he said.

"Good morning." She got a closer look at the buzz cut that Raquel gave him and reached out to touch it. "I'm glad to see that she didn't completely shave you bald."

He laughed. "Well, I'm sure she tried, but I set the razor to a specific setting for me. I cleaned it up a bit during the night. It was slightly uneven and I can understand the stares and snickers."

"Well, it suits you."

"Thank you."

"Are you ready to go down to the simulation lab?" she asked.

"Yes. I just need to finish my chart, check on Jason and then I'll come down to the simulation lab."

"Sounds good. We're ready to go and..." Emily was baffled as her pager went off and when she looked down at the number she realized it was the emergency pager for the conjoined twins.

"What is it?" Ryan asked.

"The twins. I have to go to surgery."

"Be careful. I'll be in the simulation lab, going over the nerve separation."

Emily nodded. "I'll let you know what happens."

Ryan nodded, but she could see the worry on his face. It was too early for the twins to be born and she felt the same way, but they were prepared for this. There were plans that she always had in place for premature births. She was a pediatric surgeon, but she was also a neonatologist, who dealt with preemies, and she'd delivered babies who were more premature than these twins were.

She ran as fast as she could. When she was on the operating-room floor she moved fast to change into her surgical scrubs and tied her hair back. She tossed her lab coat in a cubby and clipped her pager onto the waistband of her scrubs.

She moved quickly to the scrub room and scrubbed in before heading into the operating room.

An incubator with a warming lamp was ready, together with everything she needed for the birth of a premature infant.

Dr. Samuel was at work.

Janet had been put under because there had been no

time to wait for a spinal block to take effect as the babies were in distress.

"Glad to see you, Dr. West. I'll have the babies out momentarily," Dr. Samuel said.

"Good. I'm ready for them." Emily stepped up beside Dr. Samuel and looked down to watch the birth. The babies were small and she could see where they were joined, back to back. They would need to get stronger before they could do the separation and it would be a delicate surgery because they were so small.

She'd worked on smaller infants, but usually they weren't sharing organs with another child.

"And here we go," Dr. Samuel said as he lifted the babies up and passed them over to her. She gently held them with the help of Dr. Sharipova, who had joined her. Dr. Samuel cut and clipped the cord and one of the babies let out a weak cry, barely audible.

"Welcome to the world, little ones," Emily whispered as she and Dr. Sharipova carried them over to the incubator and laid them down.

Her surgical staff knew what to do as she got to work assessing them and giving the babies oxygen, readying them for transport up to the NICU. "Oxygen," she said, and a mask was brought. She held it over one of the babies, while Dr. Sharipova tended to the other one. The mask was too large to place over the face, but at least the baby was getting oxygen. "Dr. Teal, hold this mask."

Dr. Teal stepped up and held the mask to free up Emily's hands as she intubated the babies so they could breathe and got them hooked up to monitors.

"Okay, let's get them up to the NICU." Emily pushed the incubator to the operating-room door. She looked back to see Dr. Samuel working on the mother. A lump formed in Emily's throat as she thought about how scared that mother must've been to have been rushed off to surgery. To not know if her children were going to live or die.

Well, Emily was going to make sure that these babies were going to live. She was going to do everything in her power to make sure that the babies survived long enough to have the separation surgery and got a chance at life.

It was her job to ensure that happened, if possible.

And she was going to make it happen. No matter what.

This was not going to be a fight she was going to lose.

CHAPTER ELEVEN

RYAN HADN'T HEARD anything about the twins' birth and he paged Emily, but she wasn't answering her page, which worried him.

When he went up to the NICU he saw that the twins were in an incubator, being cared for by the nurses.

So the twins had survived the birth, which was good, but he wondered where Emily was. Her absence worried him and he hoped that she hadn't collapsed again.

"How long ago were the twins born?" Ryan asked as he picked up their chart in the NICU.

"About three hours ago," the nurse said. "Dr. West stayed until she was sure they were stable and then she went to speak to their mother, because the mother was awake and out of surgery."

Ryan nodded. "They have a brain bleed?"

"Twin A has a brain bleed. Twin B does not. B is stronger than A."

"I'm their neurosurgeon so please keep me posted on the status of twin A's brain bleed."

"Of course, Dr. Gary," the nurse said.

Ryan put the chart down and left the NICU. He had to find Emily. He paged her again, but there was still no response. His stomach twisted in a knot. He had to find her. He headed down the hall and saw one of the on-call room doors was closed, meaning there was a doctor in there, resting.

He opened the door and he could see Emily on a bed. She was sitting up, her head in her hands, and she was weeping uncontrollably.

"Hey," he said gently as he slipped into the room, shutting and locking the door behind him so that no one could walk in on them.

She looked up. Her eyes were red and there were tears streaming down her face. "Sorry."

"What do you have to be sorry about?" he asked gently sitting next to her.

"For you having to witness this. I don't know...that's not true. I know what's come over me. I'm just so angry that I'm letting it affect me. It's never bothered me before."

"What?"

"I had to talk to Janet, the mother of the conjoined twins." Emily wiped her eyes and Ryan handed her a tissue. "Thanks."

"What happened?" he asked.

"She was upset, and rightly so."

"Well, I imagine giving birth and not being able to hold your babies is devastating."

"Exactly," Emily sniffled. "And I could just feel her pain. Her absolute, gut-wrenching agony over the fact that her two little girls might die."

"Come on," Ryan said.

"What?"

"The babies are stable. Raquel is stable and you need to get rest."

"I don't want to go home to bed," she said. She took a deep, calming breath.

"Emily, you need rest."

"I need to be there for those twin girls. I'm not going to let anything happen to them!" He loved her conviction. He loved how strong she was, how much she cared about her patients. Just another reason why he adored her so much. Why he loved being around her.

"Twin A has a brain bleed," she said, sighing.

"I know."

"You know?" she asked.

"When I was went looking for you I headed up to the NICU and saw the twins. I looked over their chart and I'm monitoring the brain bleed. It's common in preemies."

"I know. I'm a neonatologist." Emily stood up, her fists clenched. "I'm so angry at myself. I deal with the sickest children. I've been to funerals that no one should ever have to attend. I've watched small lives slip through my fingers and I can hold it together. If I didn't hold it together I would've gone crazy by now. So why, why out of all the conjoined twins I have worked on, is this bothering me so much?"

"You're pregnant," Ryan said gently.

Emily rolled her eyes and then laughed. "I hate this."

"What?"

"Hormones. It's harder to keep everything under control. I get so overwhelmed."

Ryan chuckled. "We all have them…hormones, I mean, and we all have moments of feeling overwhelmed."

She glared at him, but he could see that she wasn't serious. "Men!"

"What about men?" he asked.

"You have it so easy."

"Do we? We don't," Ryan said, confused.

"Sorry," she said. "I need to get out of this hospital and I'm not going home to bed!"

"Fine. Let's go for a walk. Let's go to the Space Needle."

Emily looked at him like he was crazy. "What?"

"I said let's go to the Space Needle. Maybe the trip to the top will help you gain perspective." He stood up and walked over to her, placing his hands on her arms. "The twins are stable. The Space Needle isn't far and you need to clear your head."

He could tell she was thinking about it by the way she bit her lip and her brow was furrowed. "Fine."

"Fine?"

She nodded. "Fine, but we have to do this now!"

"Okay." He unlocked the door and opened it. "Let's get changed and we'll go for a walk. It looks to be a nice warm, almost summer night. Let's clear your head."

Thankfully, the walk to the Space Needle was exactly what Emily needed. The moment they got outside he could tell that she perked up.

He bought tickets and they took the elevator five hundred and twenty feet into the air to the observation deck. It was an impressive view from there. You could see all of Seattle, Elliott Bay and, in the distance, Mount Rainier, which they had got up close and personal with not that long ago.

"I've never been up here," Emily said contentedly.

"I'm glad you like heights."

"I'm not a fan of them, but you only live once." She wandered over to the windows that overlooked downtown Seattle and the Cascade Mountains to the east. She leaned on the railing and he was glad that the outside observation deck was closed today because of some high winds. He would feel a little bit nervous with her out there, pregnant and in high winds.

"The view is clear tonight, although there is some rain to the northeast." He pointed. "You can see the clouds coming in."

"That's not surprising. It always rains in Seattle, but I don't mind the rain. Sometimes on clear nights, if you go to the right place, you can see the Northern Lights."

He cocked an eyebrow. "Oh, really?"

She nodded. "Not often, but the first time I saw them was in my first year here in Seattle. They were over Puget Sound. It was a strong geometric storm, but they were spectacular."

"When do they show up?" Ryan asked.

"Fall."

"So not now?" he asked, slightly disappointed.

"No. Too much light."

"I haven't seen the Northern Lights in so long. It would be nice to see them again."

"It would make it perfect tonight. Maybe it would help me forget about how I lost control back there. How mad I am at myself that I couldn't keep my emotions in check."

"Did you cry in front of the patient?" Ryan asked.

"No."

"Then you kept your emotions in check. You're stronger than you think, Emily."

"I'm not that strong," she whispered. "I've just learned how to control it. To take care of myself and not to expect much from anyone."

He cocked an eyebrow. "Here I thought you'd had a happy childhood compared to mine."

"I did. I did believe in love once…"

"Was it me that changed your mind?" he asked cautiously.

"No." And even though she didn't want to talk about Robert, she was tired of carrying that burden around. She was tired of trying to hide something she was ashamed about because now, five years later, she could admit that she was ashamed that she'd fallen for a man like Robert. That he'd ruined her for all others, because she had a hard time trusting any one.

"I already told you that a bad experience had put me off surgeons forever—until you came along, that is. Well, I was involved with another surgeon during my residency years. We were both pediatric residents. I thought I was in love with him. He was wonderful and charming…"

"I hate him already on principle." Ryan winked and Emily couldn't help but chuckle as he tried to lighten the mood.

"I got promoted first and I was offered an attending position here at SMFPC, and not just any attending but head of pediatric surgery. He was livid. He belittled me because of my autism. He told me I put my work first rather than him. He was jealous, of course, but then he told me about all the women he'd slept with while we were together because I was too busy advancing my career instead of paying attention to him."

"What an ass."

"I vowed never to date or sleep with another surgeon again and I was doing fine for five years, until *you* came along." She nudged him and he laughed.

"Sorry, but really I'm not," he whispered.

Blood rushed to her cheeks and her stomach had butterflies that were not related to the baby. It was the desire, the attraction that had drawn her in six months ago. Ryan just broke down every wall she had set up.

She was vulnerable to him in way she'd never been with any other man.

To any other person.

"Well, you're not the only one who's been burned in love with a surgeon. I was in a relationship a few years ago that ended badly. She didn't like my jet-setting lifestyle and left to focus on her career. Since then I've been gun-shy."

"You're the one who didn't sign the divorce papers," Emily said, confused. "If you don't want a marriage, sign them."

"I didn't sign them because I saw you were pregnant. I didn't want to because of the baby."

"People shouldn't marry for that reason. There has to be a deeper connection and love. Marriage is forever, or at least I want to believe in forever, but…"

Ryan tilted her chin so she looked at him. His blue eyes sparkled with something that made her heart skip a beat.

Other people got off the elevator and started to walk toward them. They were loud and boisterous and it broke the spell that had been woven.

"I think I'd better go home," she said, clearing her throat.

"I'll take you home," he said. "And I won't force you to stay on bed rest."

Emily chuckled. "Deal."

Ryan was glad that those people had come, because he'd seriously wanted to take Emily in his arms up on the observation deck and kiss her again. Ever since their kiss at Mount Rainier National Park, he hadn't been able to stop thinking about it, but he was trying.

She deserved so much better than him.

He got her back to her apartment and even though he knew he shouldn't go up, she invited him and he went.

Part of him was telling him to go and take a chance with Emily and the other part of him was reminding him how he was unreliable when it came to relationships and he shouldn't lead her on. The thing was, he falling so hard for her. He just wasn't sure that his heart could take hurting her or having her walk away from him.

He was too afraid.

They sat together on the couch, watching a movie, but he wasn't really paying attention to the movie at all. All he could think about was how close she was. He could smell the scent of her shampoo, feel the warmth of her body.

"Ryan," she whispered.

"Yes."

"Why don't we give it a trial run?"

"Give what a trial run?" he asked.

"The marriage. I mean, we're married and we have to get to know each other, but why don't we try for the baby's sake? If it doesn't work out, we walk away."

It was everything he wanted to hear, but he was too afraid to reach out and grasp it.

"Em, I…"

She touched his face, tears in her eyes. "I—I want to try, Ryan. I don't know where this is going, but I want to try. I'm just afraid of making a mistake again."

"I'm not like him. I would never hurt you."

"You did when you didn't respond to those emails."

He sighed and brushed back her hair from her forehead. "I never meant to hurt you, Em. I swear to you that I didn't get them, or I would've come."

Would you?

"I believe you. Part of me says not to, but I do believe you. I trust you, which is hard for me."

Ryan brushed his hand across her cheek. Her skin was so soft. "I'm sorry. I didn't know. I'm sorry you were alone for so long."

She laid her head against his should and he drank in her scent. Coconuts.

She deserved so much better than him, but she was giving him a chance to have everything he'd ever wanted but had been too afraid to reach out and take.

"I'm happy, Em." He placed his hand on her belly. "Truly."

Her eyes filled with tears. "I like it when you hold me like this."

"And I like it too." The baby pushed back, a strong kick against his palm, and he couldn't help but smile at that little life reaching out to him. "He or she is getting stronger."

"I know. They keep me up at night. He or she is troublesome. Like you," she teased.

Ryan chuckled and tilted her chin. Those blue eyes of hers and those soft pink lips... He was so in love with her, though he didn't deserve it. He leaned in and kissed her, just like he'd wanted to do on the observation deck of the Space Needle. He wanted her again, but he knew one more stolen moment with her would never be enough.

"Oh, Ryan," she whispered against his lips.

"Em, I..."

"I want you too." She kissed him again. "I want you so much."

She was saying yes and that was all he needed. Even though he shouldn't, he was drunk on her and couldn't resist her. He scooped her up in his arms and carried her to her bedroom.

He didn't want to rush anything because he didn't want to hurt her. He set her down on the floor and cupped her face to kiss her again. Ryan couldn't get enough of her kisses. He helped her out of her clothes, which weren't much. Just a sweater and a pair of sweatpants. He lifted her sweater over her head and undid her bra. And as he helped her out of her sweatpants he laid kisses along her abdomen and lower, making her moan with pleasure.

"Your turn," she whispered as he stood up. She undid his shirt. He loved the feel of her hands on his chest.

"I've missed you," she whispered as he held her in his arms.

"I've missed you too."

And he had. She was all he'd been thinking about since their night in Vegas together.

Emily led him to her bed and sat down on the edge as she guided him down beside her. They sat on the bed, kissing and touching. He couldn't think straight. He just focused on the sounds of pleasure Emily was making and that was enough to make his blood heat.

Emily's moans were all that mattered to him tonight.

Emily wanted this to happen. She was glad the kiss had happened. For one brief moment she wanted to be happy. She wanted to be blissfully unaware and not worried about what tomorrow might bring.

Right now, she wanted to feel.

To taste passion in his arms one more time, because even though she offered him her heart and a chance at a family, she wasn't sure that it would work. She knew that he was still running from something. There was something more, but right now she just wanted this stolen moment.

His mouth opened against her as she kissed him, his kiss deepening. His hands felt hot on her bare back, searching over her skin and driving her wild with need.

He pushed her down on the mattress, lying beside her. Ryan brought out desire in her she'd never felt with another.

She craved him and that thought scared her because tomorrow he might leave. He'd said he wouldn't, but it was an uncertainty. She was treading on dangerous ground but right now she couldn't care less.

The kiss ended, leaving her quivering with desire.

"Oh, Em. I want you so much," he whispered against her neck.

A tingle of anticipation ran through her. She remembered his touch, the way he felt inside her. The way he made her feel when she came around him.

"So beautiful," he murmured, his hand touching her.

When he kissed her again, it was urgent against her lips as he drew her body against his. His lips trailed down her neck to her breasts and she arched against his mouth on her nipples. The pleasure it brought her was something she'd never experienced before. Her body was more sensitive to his touch now.

"I want you, Ryan."

"I'll be gentle, Em. Please tell me if I hurt you. I don't want that."

"You won't hurt me. I just want this moment with you."

Ryan stroked her cheek and his hand trailed down over her abdomen, lower, touching her intimately. Her body thrummed with desire. She wanted more. So much more.

Their gazes locked as he entered her. He nipped her neck and moved slowly. She wrapped her arms around his neck. She wanted all of him. She wanted him deeper, wanted it hard and fast.

She felt alive.

She was in love with him and she was scared by the way he made her feel, but she didn't care about that at this moment. She wanted to savor it.

He quickened his pace and she climaxed fast, crying out as pleasure flooded through her veins. It wasn't long until he joined her.

Ryan kissed the top of her head and held her close. She didn't want this moment to end. She never wanted him to leave.

It scared her how much she wanted him.

It scared her how comfortable she was in his arms, that soon she forgot about all her worries, all her fears and her own self-doubt. She couldn't think straight with his strong arms wrapped around her. Her body relaxed, she was warm and safe with him. Safe with a man she wasn't sure was going to be here the next day, but she didn't care as sleep overtook her and she fell into a relaxed and blissfully deep slumber.

CHAPTER TWELVE

SOMETHING IS NOT right today. Something is different.

For two weeks everything had been running smoothly. Ryan had left his hotel suite and temporarily moved in with her. During the day they worked with their patients and at night they went home and spent the evenings wrapped up in each other's arms.

They didn't talk about the next day.

They just lived in the moment and, for the most part, Emily was happy with this arrangement, but there was a part of her, that niggling self-doubt, that worried that he wouldn't really stay. That her baby would grow up without a dad. That she was falling for someone who would hurt her in the end.

And every time she thought about that she got emotional and that was the last thing she needed.

The conjoined twins, Sasha and Melanie, were stable and getting stronger. Every day they lived, every day they were stable put them one day closer to a successful separation surgery and that gave her hope.

Every day they practiced the simulation in the sim lab, until they had the procedure down to an art with all the surgeons who would be involved. Ryan would practice in the lab with different scenarios of nerve bundles.

As Emily did her rounds, she had a nagging feeling that today was going to be different. That they had been in this holding pattern for far too long and, much like a volcano, it was only a matter of time before something burst.

"You okay?" Ryan asked when she stopped at the nurses' station on the general pediatric floor. "You look tense."

"Something feels off."

He cocked any eyebrow. "Don't say the Q word, you know that brings down wrath."

She chuckled. "I wouldn't and usually that's only in the emergency room."

"Well, it's best not to say it anyway."

"How did your simulation go?" she asked.

"Good. I think, based on their last scans, I know how to tackle it. Once you've done your part and we flip them, I'll separate the nerves at the base of their spines. I have a graft for Sasha, because most of the tailbone is on Melanie's side. Given their young age, the graft should work well."

Emily nodded but bit her lip, worrying. There was something not right. She heard a crack of thunder and looked up at the skylight in the hall where they were standing. It became dark, really fast. A storm was moving in. There was a flash of lightning.

"Perhaps that's your sense of foreboding," Ryan said, pointing at the skylight with his pen.

"I hope you're right." And as soon as she said those words her pager went off.

Her heart sank as she saw it was from the NICU.

It was the twins.

She didn't explain but took off running, dodging people in the hall as she made her way to the NICU. Ryan was right behind her, having received the page too.

"Get Dr. Sharipova to ready the operating room and get your neuro team ready," she shouted as she got on the elevator.

Ryan nodded. "I'll see you down there."

Emily pushed the button. The elevator door closed slowly, or what felt like slowly. She just hoped that she would see him down there. That she was able to stabilize them.

When she got to the NICU Janet was standing outside, tears streaming down her face because they had kicked her out while the babies were in distress.

"Dr. West," Janet sobbed. "My girls."

"I'm going to have to do the separation now. I wanted them older and stronger, but if I don't do the surgery now, they won't survive. Do you consent?"

Janet nodded. Her husband had his arms on her shoulder and he was trembling.

"We'll update you as soon as possible." Emily squirted hand sanitizer on her hands and headed into the NICU. There was a flurry of nurses and neonatologist residents working on the girls.

"What do we have?" Emily shouted over the commotion.

"Tachycardia in twin B and twin A's organs are beginning to shut down. Their shared kidneys are trying to keep up, but it's too much. Also the creatinine is high. They're overworked and they're in threat of going into multisystem organ failure."

Emily nodded and went to work, getting the babies ready to transport down to the operating room. "I want all available neonatologist residents in operating room three. I need as many hands as I can. We have practiced this surgery, now it's time to turn practice into reality."

"Of course, Dr. West," one of the NICU nurses said. Emily couldn't see her face as she worked on the babies. Once she was sure they were stable enough, they hooked up all the leads and monitors to travel and pushed the incubator out of the NICU and straight to the patient transfer elevator.

Emily tried not to look at Janet. She knew that if she looked at Janet crying she would lose control of her carefully guarded emotions because, as she looked down at the two little girls clinging to life, she couldn't help but think of her own baby.

And how she would feel if she were in Janet's shoes.

She hoped that she was never in Janet's shoes.

She hoped that she never had to be in the place most parents were when they had a seriously ill child.

You've got this.

Sasha and Melanie were not going to die today.

When they entered the operating-room floor she left the babies to get ready. There was a flurry of doctors and nurses getting ready to scrub in as the babies were taken to the operating room. Emily tied on her favorite scrub cap and headed to the scrub room.

The gallery was filling with interns and the chief of surgery was watching, waiting. It was overwhelming. She hated crowds, but at least they weren't in the operating room with her. She could drown them out.

Emily took a deep, calming breath.

You've got this.

She looked down at her belly when her baby kicked. "Listen, we need to talk before I go in there. This will be a long surgery. I know it will be hard on us, but we have to do this."

There was no response, so Emily took that as an affirmative her baby would behave and it relaxed her to be just a bit silly, talking to her child.

Ryan was in the operating room already, directing the surgical staff as they came in. The babies were being transferred from the incubator to two operating tables. They were so tiny as they were placed between the two large tables. Once they were separated the two teams would work hard to close the incisions and repair any damage.

The most stressful part of this surgery would be turning the babies so that Ryan could work on their spines.

You've got this.

Emily entered the operating room and a scrub nurse helped her into a surgical gown. Her heart was racing as she looked at those little lives on the operating room table.

Breathe.

The babies were put under and she directed her team to Melanie, while the other pediatric surgeon was working on Sasha. Ryan stood on the sidelines. She glanced up at him and he nodded. His eyes were crinkled and she knew that he was smiling, encouraging her to keep going, that she had this. It was exactly what she needed.

"All right, teams. This is what we practiced for. This is the separation of the conjoined twins Melanie and Sasha Wainwright. I will be working on twin B and Dr. Knox will be working on twin A. After we have separated them down to the spines, we will do a very careful flip and Dr. Gary will take over to separate them at the tailbone, hopefully keeping their nerves intact so that they will have full function. Let's get started."

Emily stepped up to the table.

She looked down at those babies. So helpless.

I've got you.

"Scalpel."

Her body was aching, but the baby hadn't kicked her and she was glad for that. Separation surgeries were long. After she had done her part and they were able to flip the babies, she could sit down and let Ryan take over.

And after several hours, she was almost ready to do the flip.

Twin A, Melanie, had two kidneys because the one kidney she had was too small and the shared kidney was regular size. Twin B, Sasha, had one kidney now, but it was a strong one. The bowels had been successfully resected and repaired and the liver had been separated. The only thing holding them back now was the tailbone and the nerves at the end of the spines.

"Are you good, Dr. Knox?" Emily asked.

"I am good. You, Dr. West?"

"I'm ready for the flip and for Dr. Gary to take over."

More than ready.

She needed to sit down and she needed a protein shake so that she could keep going. She could leave, but she wanted to see this through to the end.

"Okay, teams. Carefully." They had surgeons holding the babies, covering their open incision and making sure all their tubes, their IVs and everything else flipped correctly. Emily held her breath as she held the babies too. More hands, keeping everything steady, would help insure a successful flip. It was like trying not to crush a snowflake in your hand. It was so delicate.

"And the flip is successful!" Emily said in relief.

There was applause from the gallery.

She took a step back as Ryan and his neurosurgical team took over.

Emily sat down on a stool and Dr. Teal handed her a protein shake and then mopped her head.

"Excellent work, Dr. West," Amanda said.

Emily smiled weakly up at her. "It's not over yet."

She watched as Ryan focused on his work. There were sensors monitoring nerve impulses. Emily kept her eyes trained on them. Watching the monitor gave her a sense of calm. Even if one twin couldn't walk, it was still a victory.

Emily was just hoping for a perfect score.

She worried her lip. Watching the monitor was easier than watching the clock.

"Dr. Teal, give the Wainwrights an update on their daughters. Tell them the flip was successful."

"Yes, Dr. West." Amanda left the operating room. It would be some time before Ryan finished his work. Dr. Teal wouldn't miss the final surgeries. Emily glanced to the side of the operating room where two incubators waited so they could transport the twins up to the NICU.

Come on.

She closed her eyes and sent up a silent prayer.

This had to work.

"Twin A, both legs are working, as are the arms," Ryan announced after some time. There was applause again and her heart skipped a beat. This was the end of the separation, but she held her breath, watching the second monitor.

Come on, Sasha. Come on.

"Twin B, both legs and arms are working. Well done, team!" Ryan said, and she could hear the relief in his voice. "The twins are successfully separated."

There was more applause as the tables were separated and Emily moved quickly to work on Twin A, Melanie, who was having a rough start. Dr. Knox knew what he was doing and he took over the other twin. Emily had to put Sasha out of her head to focus on Melanie. She glanced up to see Ryan leaving the operating room. His job here was done.

She nodded and then turned back to her work.

"How are we doing?" Emily asked.

"Her stats are improving," Dr. Sharipova said.

"Come over here, Dr. Teal, and hold this retractor." Emily knew Dr. Teal had earned the right and she deserved to see it up close. Dr. Teal had been her right-hand man lately.

"Thank you, Dr. West." Amanda took the retractor and they worked on closing Melanie's incisions. The babies were no longer dependent on each other and it would take some time, they weren't out of the woods yet, but their little bodies were beginning to respond as there wasn't as much demand on their organs.

Emily finished closing. "Let's get her transferred to the incubator and up to the NICU. Do you think you can handle that, Dr. Sharipova?"

"Yes, Dr. West." Dr. Sharipova went to scrub out as Emily and the rest of her team transferred Melanie to her incubator. She was stable and now the next twenty-four hours would tell the real tale.

Emily glanced over at Dr. Knox and his team was placing Sasha into her incubator.

Emily breathed a sigh of relief and took a seat.

"Job well done, everyone."

There was further applause and she glanced up into the gallery. Interns were starting to leave and the chief of surgery gave her a thumbs-up.

The babies were taken out of the operating room and all that was left was an empty space. Emily took off her mask and discarded her surgical gown. She couldn't leave the operating room right away. She needed a moment, just a moment to herself in the calm after the storm to cry.

It was done.

Now she needed to regain her composure and let a very worried mother know that her babies had survived their surgery.

Ryan's hands were still shaking as he headed back up to the neurosurgical pediatric ward. He'd received a page about Jason and he needed to attend to that. He was trying to not let his nerves get the better of him.

He'd done conjoined separations before. He'd worked on aneurysms and delicate spinal cords. He'd worked on some of the most delicate structures, but nothing had compared to that. Nothing compared to separating those tiny babies and knowing that if he messed up somehow Emily might not forgive him.

He scrubbed a hand over his face and he tried to not let his emotions get the better of him. He tried not to think about his baby. The baby he hadn't got to see.

He'd been almost afraid to touch the twins for fear of hurting them. What kind of person was afraid of touching an infant? What kind of surgeon was he that he was so afraid of working on an infant, because every time he looked down at a baby all he could think about was the one he'd lost.

All he could think about was the irrational part of him that didn't want to be like his father.

And, truth be told, he'd loved the two weeks he'd been living with Emily, but he was needed for a consult back in New York City and he wanted to go.

That's because you're a coward and running. Always running from responsibility on the off chance you might get hurt.

So like his father. Selfish. Never putting down roots.

Ryan hated himself for it.

When he got to Jason's room he saw a flurry of activity and Jason's parents were nowhere to be found. Ryan's stomach dropped to the soles of his feet and he ran into Jason's room. And all he could think about was the fact that he'd done therapeutic hypothermia on Jason and it had been his first time doing that procedure on a child younger than twelve.

Perhaps Emily was right and he'd done something horrible.

It was something he thought about all the time. Every day when he went to check on Jason and saw no improvement in his paralysis it weighed heavily on him. Perhaps he had made a dreadful mistake.

"What's going on?"

"He coded. He stopped breathing and we had to intubate him," the resident said. "We got him back, but his stats are low and there is a bruising and rigidity in his abdomen. We think the spleen might've ruptured."

"Let's get him to the operating room." Ryan cursed himself inwardly. It might be a clot somewhere and that's why he was bleeding out. Something that had been missed because he'd just been focusing on the spine. It could've been missed and he was slowly dying inside from a nick.

You're an arrogant fool.

He should've listened to Emily.

As they were wheeling Jason down the hall, Emily was coming up from the operating-room floor. Her eyes widened as she saw them and she rushed over to them.

"What happened?"

"Internal bleeding. Looks like the spleen, but we don't know. He needs an exploratory laparotomy. He coded and they had to intubate." Ryan could see the anger in her eyes, but there were too many people around and she didn't say anything to him. She just took a place beside the gurney and helped them get down to the operating-room floor, but he knew what she was thinking.

She was thinking back to that moment when he'd first arrived in Seattle, when she'd reamed him out for doing the therapeutic hypothermia. He knew that's what she was thinking. He could see it in her expression.

Jason was taken to an operating room and they headed into the scrub room. Emily still wasn't saying anything. She was scrubbing, but he could tell she was stressed and tired. She'd just done a separation of conjoined twins and he was worried that she was pushing herself too hard.

"I'm going to call Dr. Knox," Ryan said firmly. "You shouldn't be doing this exploratory laparotomy."

"I wouldn't have to do this if you hadn't done what you did," she snapped.

Ryan got angry. "You don't know if that's the cause. There are a lot of things that could've happened. His white cell count is up, it could be an infection."

"You made a risky decision and Jason is going to

pay for it!" She toweled off and headed into the operating room.

It was like a slap across the face.

She was right and he had made a bad decision that had put this boy in jeopardy. Every day that Jason didn't regain movement made him realize that his choice, in that moment when he had first been injured, had been wrong.

You're only human.

He entered the operating room and his stomach was in knots as Emily stepped up to the operating table. He could see her sway as she asked for a scalpel and began the surgery.

"I will take over until Dr. Knox arrives," Ryan said firmly. "You need to leave this operating room."

"I'm not leaving. I am the head of pediatric surgery and I've started the procedure." And she had. Jason was lying open on the table.

"And I am this patient's doctor. Dr. Knox will do the exploratory surgery and you will get out of my operating room." He hated speaking to her so firmly.

"I will not. I have control—"

"Look, I know your Asperger's makes it hard for to relinquish control, but you will this time. He's my patient and you need to leave my operating room. Now!"

He regretted the words as soon as he'd said them.

He could see the hurt in her eyes. The shock of the others who hadn't known she was on the spectrum. He'd betrayed her trust.

He was a monster.

"I'm not…" Her eyes rolled back and she collapsed to the floor.

"Page Dr. Samuel!" Ryan moved to grab her, but then Jason's monitors went off and he had to start the surgery.

If there was internal bleeding he had to put a stop to it. He couldn't leave the patient, so he had to leave Emily, lying unconscious on the floor.

"Get her out of here and page Dr. Samuel."

A couple of residents came in with a stretcher and laid Emily on it, placing an oxygen mask over her face as she was rushed from the operating room.

He felt like a failure as two lives were in jeopardy and he felt completely helpless.

Again.

CHAPTER THIRTEEN

RYAN HADN'T COME to see her last night.

Dr. Samuel told her he'd paged him, but Ryan hadn't come and it was her fault. She'd snapped at him about his decision and she knew logically that wasn't the reason that Jason had coded. She had just been angry that Jason had coded and she had been exhausted.

And she had known deep down that the day was going to be bad. The surgeries had turned out well, but she might've ruined things with Ryan. She'd lorded her position over him and he'd, rightfully, booted her out of his operating room. Still, what he'd said to her in front of the others had hurt. He'd betrayed her trust.

She should've known. She should've stayed away from him like every gut instinct in her body had screamed at her to do. Surgeons did not make good life partners. At least in her case. All surgeons, herself included, had God complexes. They were egotistical and some surgeons couldn't handle a woman being in power.

She'd thought that Ryan was different.

Clearly, she had been wrong.

At least the babies had made it through the night and were stable. That was a consolation prize, but she didn't know how Jason was doing.

She wiped away a tear and wished she could take back what she'd said to Ryan. She wished she hadn't pushed herself too hard, because Dr. Samuel had made it clear that her maternity leave was starting now.

There was a knock on the door and she glanced over to see Ryan hovering there.

There were dark circles under his eyes and her heart sank as she thought of their patient.

"Oh, no, you didn't lose him, did you?" she asked.

"No," he said, but he didn't come closer. "Part of his bowel had died and his spleen had a small tear that was fixed. Part of his bowel was resected. He should make a full recovery."

"Good." She expected him to come into the room and sit down next to her, but he stood in the doorway and was unable to look at her. He couldn't handle her. He couldn't handle her being on the spectrum, of being a head attending. He was going to leave. Just like she'd thought he would at the beginning. The problem was her heart was involved now.

Even more so.

"I've been called to New York."

Her heart sank. "Oh?"

"A consult and I'm needed there."

"You're not staying." It was like a stab to the heart, but it wasn't unexpected.

"No… I can't… I can't handle this, Em."

Tears streamed down her face. "I should've known."

"What's that supposed to mean?"

"You can't handle a woman in authority either. You can't handle that I might be a better surgeon than you. You want a demure pushover and I'm not that person. I've never been that person. I've worked hard to get where I am and…yeah, I should've known better than to think that another relationship with a surgeon would go well."

"That's not it," he snapped. "That's not it at all."

"What're you running from, then?" she demanded. "What're you so afraid of?"

Ryan wouldn't look at her and it broke her heart.

She was in love with him. She had never felt this way about Robert. She had been hurt when he'd turned his back on her, but this tore her in two. She loved Ryan so much, but it was better that he walk away now before their child got hurt too.

"I'm sorry, Em."

"You're not. It's why you told everyone I struggle with my diagnosis. You're ashamed about it too. Well, I'm not. Not anymore. So you did me a favor. My only mistake was letting you into my life." Her lips trembled. "Just go. I was a fool."

She wouldn't look at him and she tried so hard to keep the tears from falling. She didn't want him to see her like this, weak and exposed. Vulnerable and heart-broken.

"Goodbye, Emily."

She heard the door shut and wept. When she looked back she saw the divorce papers, signed and sitting on the table next to her bed.

So it was done.

And she knew she was never going to love anyone else again.

All she had was her baby and that was good enough.

It would just be her and her child against the world.

The way it was supposed to be the day she'd found out she was pregnant.

* * *

You're the worst person ever.

His heart was breaking. He had almost killed a patient with his foolhardy decision. The hypothermia hadn't corrected the paralysis and the paralysis had caused a world of problems and more surgeries.

And then Emily had collapsed after he'd betrayed her trust and he'd thought he was going to lose them both. Dr. Samuel had told him she was on bed rest for the rest of her pregnancy. He was told the baby might come early if she kept pushing herself and he couldn't bear the thought of losing them.

Of losing their child.

He scrubbed his hand over his face as he collected his things from the attendings' lounge. He left his hospital identification in the locker.

You could stay.

Only he didn't think that was a good choice. Working on children was too hard. He couldn't handle working on broken, fragile bodies. He was going to focus on adults.

He was tired of losses.

He was too afraid to take any more chances with young lives.

He was too afraid that he would end up like his father.

You already have. You're just like your father. You're running. Always running.

What was he doing? Why was he so afraid to take a chance?

He knew the reason. He was so afraid of losing everything. He was so afraid of reliving the pain. Not just the pain of losing that child that Morgan had briefly carried but losing his family. He was so afraid of the unknown when it came to family and love.

Life was this horrible complicated thing. It came with pain and joy. He didn't know what the future held, but he couldn't walk away from Emily and the baby.

He loved them too much. He loved Emily so much it scared him. The way she was, all she'd had to overcome only made him respect and love her more. The thought of losing her was too much to bear. The thought of hurting her ate away at him.

He couldn't leave.

He had been a fool for running for so long. He wasn't going to walk away from Emily, the woman he loved. He may have hurt her, but he'd spend the rest of his life making it up to her. If she'd let him.

There was a page for Jason's room and he set down his things and headed back there, fearing the worst but knowing he had to face the music. He'd seen the pain in Jason's parents' eyes, the pain in all the parents' eyes when they thought their child was going to die. When they looked over the edge into the black abyss of death.

He'd been there.

Instead of the flurry of nurses and the sound of a code, he saw Jason's parents crying and his stomach twisted. *Oh, God. No.*

And just as he thought the worst he saw that Jason's parents were also smiling through the tears and laughing! Ryan walked into the room to find Jason was awake.

"Doc!" Jason said. "I wanted you to see this."

"See what?" Ryan asked.

Jason wiggled his toes on his left foot and his right foot rose a bit. "I can feel them. I can move them."

A sense of relief washed over him.

It had worked. He hadn't ruined this child's life. His

crazy leap of faith had saved his life. Ryan pulled out a discriminator and ran it over Jason's right foot.

"Can you feel that?"

"Yeah," Jason said excitedly. "Barely, but I can."

Jason's mother sobbed and Ryan couldn't help but smile. "Well, it's going to take some time, but this is a good sign, Jason. A good sign."

Jason smiled and his mother leaned over and kissed her son.

"Thank you, Dr. Gary," Jason's father said. "I thought... we thought... Thank you for saving his life. That was the scariest moment of my life."

"It's up there for me too," Ryan admitted.

Ryan watched the family holding each other. They were so happy. He had to tell Emily. He had to see her.

He went to her room and she was lying on her side, her back to the door. He could see a box of tissues in front of her, next to the divorce papers that he planned to tear up.

"Emily," he said as he slipped into the room.

"Go away," she sniffled.

"No."

She rolled over and looked at him like he was crazy. "What do you mean, no? You're the one who walked away from me. You're the one who signed the divorce papers. I know I sent them to you, but that was before—"

"I know. And you're right, I was running from something, but it has nothing to do with your work."

"Really?" she asked skeptically.

"Really. I don't have a problem with you being head of pediatric surgery. I don't care that you yelled at me about my treatment plan. I don't care that you're on the spectrum. You're right, we're egotistical surgeons. We're robots, except when it comes to the people we love. And

I love you, Emily. I was just too afraid to allow myself to love you."

"Because of your father? Ryan, you don't have to be like him and I don't think you could be like him."

"No, it's not because of him. I was afraid of losing you and losing our baby. I was afraid of losing another child and being powerless to stop it."

Her eyes widened. "Another child?"

Ryan sat down next to her. "That relationship I was in. She became pregnant but she didn't tell me. She was very focused on her career, as was I at the time, and she'd obviously decided that a baby was going to get in her way. I was away on a consult. When I returned it was to find that she'd left me and she had terminated the pregnancy I didn't even know she was carrying. I wasn't there. I wasn't involved in her decision. It was her decision and I knew she didn't want a baby, but she wouldn't give me the choice. She took that choice from me. It crushed me.

"If I kept running I didn't have to feel the pain." His voice caught. "I'm tired of running, Em, and I'm scared about what the future holds, but I can't keep running. I love you too much and I was a fool."

Emily touched his face. "Yes, you're a fool. And I love you too. I was so afraid of having my heart broken again I didn't want to let you in, but you made me realize that love is real and possible."

"I'm sorry I hurt you, and if you've already signed the papers then we can get remarried."

"I didn't."

"Good." Ryan picked them up and tore them in half. He kissed Emily on top of her head. "I love you. I love you so much it terrifies me beyond reason."

"I love you too. I thought I could do this on my own…"

"You could."

"But I don't want to. I want you in my life, in our daughter's life."

Ryan smiled and reached down to touch her belly. "A girl."

"Yes. Before he put me on bed rest Dr. Samuel did an ultrasound to check that all was well with the baby. That's when he asked me if I wanted to know what we were having."

He touched her face and kissed her. "I love you and I love our precious daughter. I have even more good news for you."

"Oh?"

"Jason's toes are moving."

Emily sighed. "That's wonderful. So it worked. I'm sorry for questioning you."

"You're a surgeon. It's what we do."

"What about the consult in New York City?" she asked.

"They can find someone else or come here. I'm taking up your chief's offer to work here in Seattle. I like it here and I know you're comfortable here. This is where I want to stay."

"You want to live here and work here with me?" she asked in disbelief.

"Yes, and we can still argue if we don't agree with each other's treatment plans for patients," he teased.

Emily laughed and kissed him. "I swear I'll lay off you if you come to work here."

"Don't. How else are we going to have a chance to make up? Making up is the best part." And he pulled her close, never wanting to let her go.

EPILOGUE

One year later, Seattle

IT WAS A beautiful spring day and Emily was glad to finally get out and get some much-needed vitamin D. It had been so gloomy the last few days in Seattle. Usually she liked the rain, but then again when she was working she never really paid attention to the weather.

She was still on maternity leave and when their daughter Ruth was sleeping she was bored out of her mind, watching the rain. So she was glad to see the sun.

And it would be nice to visit the hospital and see Ryan. Truth be told, Emily was itching to get back to work. So with the sunny day it was a perfect excuse to walk from their apartment and visit Ryan at work.

Their daughter, Ruth, was sleeping in her stroller, but every time Emily brought her by everyone made a fuss over her, so she never did get much sleep when they visited SMFPC.

She was glad she'd been able to take a whole year off to spend time with her. Although she did miss work, but her practice was in good hands with Dr. Sharipova having just passed his boards to become an attending at

SMFPC. Her practice was well taken care of, though it had been hard to let go of her control.

She'd have it back soon enough when she returned—and, besides, right now the baby was boss!

Ryan was waiting by the front doors. He beamed at them when they entered the hospital and Emily was surprised to see him there, waiting. She'd told him that they would stop by, but usually when she stopped by with Ruth she'd have to page him, because she never knew where he was going to be.

"I thought you would be upstairs on the neuro floor?" Emily asked.

"Not today." And he smiled like he had a secret. She hated secrets and he knew that.

Ryan bent down and gave their almost one-year-old daughter a kiss on the top of her head. "I miss her when I'm at work."

"I know," Emily said dryly. "Now, tell me what the secret is."

"What secret?" he asked innocently.

"I can tell that you're hiding something from me. You know that secrets drive me bonkers."

"But you're handling them so well. Remember when I flew your parents in from Salt Lake City to celebrate Christmas? You loved that."

Emily crossed her arms. "What is the secret, Ryan? What're you hiding from me?"

"Come upstairs to the conference room."

"Conference room?" Now she was really curious to know what was going on.

Ryan just grinned, but he wouldn't say anything. They took the elevator up to the top floor where there were several staff members waiting for her.

Dr. Teal, who was now a resident, gave her a quick hug and Dr. Samuel was also there. Behind him was Dr. Ruchi.

"Ana!" Emily gave her mentor a hug. "You hate traveling. What are you doing here in Seattle?"

"Well, I had to accompany some very special patients here."

Emily's heart skipped a beat and Ryan pushed the stroller as Ana took Emily's arm and led her into the conference room.

The first person she noticed standing by the door was a very mature-looking preteen, whose dark curly hair had grown back.

"Raquel!" Emily gasped.

Raquel beamed. "Dr. West!"

Vanessa, Raquel's mother, gave Emily a hug. "Thank you, Dr. West. If you hadn't been there that day in the bistro and sent Raquel to SMFPC I don't think we'd be here today."

Emily's eyes filled with tears and she shot Ryan a look, but he still looked all innocent.

The next was a boy, who was standing with the aid of metal braces and a cane.

"You didn't work on me long, but Dr. Gary wanted me to be here so you can see how far I've come."

"Jason. It's good to see you." Emily brushed a tear away and Ana led her to the last patients. Two blonde toddlers rushing around the room and Emily broke down in tears. It was Melanie and Sasha, the conjoined twins. The case that had brought her and Ryan back together again.

Janet Wainwright had tears in her eyes too. "Thank you, Dr. West."

Emily spun around and looked at Ryan, who was holding their daughter. "What is this all about?"

"It's been a year since we decided to take a chance and become a family and these are the patients that we worked on, argued over and saved together. Just like you saved my life. I love you, Em, and I know you've been missing work, being on maternity leave."

Emily laughed and wiped the tears from her eyes. She stood on tiptoe and kissed Ryan. "Thank you."

"You're welcome. Thank you for being my wife, for having our daughter and for just being a genuinely awesome surgeon. Here's to more lives saved when you get back."

"Here, here," Dr. Ruchi concurred. "Now, let's have some of this cake."

Emily leaned her head against her husband's shoulder as Ana served up the cake. Emily had never thought that she could be this happy. She'd never believed in love, not really. Or at least she hadn't believed in love for herself.

Thankfully she had been mistaken, because love had found her. She'd thought that no one would understand the way she saw the world. That no one would get her, but Ryan did. She had the love of Ryan, their daughter and love surrounded her in her work. Sadness too, but it was the wins that mattered. And in this moment, surrounded by those patients that brought her and Ryan together, she was very much reminded of the power of wins.

The power of love.

She was happy.

Blissfully happy, and she was so thankful that she'd decided to take a chance and let Ryan in. She hadn't appreciated it at first when she'd got pregnant after their fling in Las Vegas, but she was glad that she'd chosen to throw caution to the wind and take a chance on Ryan.

She was glad she hadn't played it safe that night and had lived a bit, that she'd conquered all her fears and overcome every obstacle that had been set in her path.

If she hadn't, she wouldn't be here today.

She wouldn't have her family.

She wouldn't have love, and a life without love was a life she didn't want to live.

* * * * *

COMING SOON!

We really hope you enjoyed reading this book. If you're looking for more romance, be sure to head to the shops when new books are available on

Thursday 21st February

To see which titles are coming soon, please visit

millsandboon.co.uk/nextmonth

MILLS & BOON

Coming next month

A WIFE FOR THE SURGEON SHEIKH
Meredith Webber

Malik saw what little colour she'd had in her cheeks fade, and the tip of her tongue slide across her pale lips.

And found himself wanting nothing more than to take care of her—this small, fiercely protective woman. Not only to keep her safe but to lift the burden of fear from her slim shoulders.

To hold her, tell her it would all work out.

To hold her?

Get your mind back on the job.

But guilt at how he'd hurt her with his words made him reach out and touch one small, cold hand, where it lay in her lap.

'I'm sorry, I shouldn't have threatened you like that—you look exhausted, and all this has been a shock to you. No one should make decisions when they're tired, but there's a way out of this for all of us. Don't answer now, we will talk again in the morning. I shall phone your Mr Marshall and explain you won't be in to work.'

But she'd obviously stopped listening earlier in his conversation.

'A way out for all of us?' she asked, looking at him with a thousand questions in her lovely eyes.

'Of course,' he told her, and felt a small spurt of unexpected excitement even thinking about his solution.

'We shall get married,' he announced. 'That way Nim is both of ours and will be doubly protected.'

Her eyes had widened and although he hadn't thought she could get any paler, she was now sheet-white.

She stood up, and for a moment he thought she might physically attack him, but in the end she glared at him, and said, 'You must be mad!' before disappearing down the passage, presumably into her bedroom.

Malik realised there was no point in arguing, but the idea, which had come to him out of nowhere, was brilliant.

All he had to do was convince Lauren.

Her name rolled a little on his tongue and, inside his head, he tried it out a few times.

And his mind, for once, was not on Nimr, but on the woman he'd decided to marry…

Continue reading
A WIFE FOR THE SURGEON SHEIKH
Meredith Webber

Available next month
www.millsandboon.co.uk

LET'S TALK
Romance

For exclusive extracts, competitions
and special offers, find us online: